## "There's a piece of unfinished business between us, Viola."

Stephen inclined his head in the direction of her bed. "And we just happen to be in the perfect place to finish it."

His fingertips burned through the fragile silk of her dress as they moved over her collarbone to the primly fastened neckline. He unbuttoned the top button.

She tried not to panic at the rush of anticipation she experienced. Her body, once again, was reacting to him...

"You must be out of your mind," she said desperately.

Dear Reader:

Three months ago we were delighted to announce the arrival of TO HAVE AND TO HOLD, the thrilling new romance series that takes you into the world of married love. We're pleased to report that letters of praise and enthusiasm are pouring in daily. TO HAVE AND TO HOLD is clearly off to a great start!

TO HAVE AND TO HOLD is the first and only series that portrays the joys and heartaches of marriage. Its unique concept makes it significantly different from the other lines now available to you, and it presents stories that meet the high standards set by SECOND CHANCE AT LOVE. TO HAVE AND TO HOLD offers all the compelling romance, exciting sensuality, and heartwarming entertainment you expect.

We think you'll love TO HAVE AND TO HOLD—and that you'll become the kind of loyal reader who is making SECOND CHANCE AT LOVE an ever-increasing success. Read about love affairs that last a lifetime. Look for three TO HAVE AND TO HOLD romances each and every month, as well as six SECOND CHANCE AT LOVE romances each month. We hope you'll read and enjoy them all. And please keep writing! Your thoughts about our books are very important to us.

Warm wishes,

*Ellen Edwards*

Ellen Edwards
SECOND CHANCE AT LOVE
The Berkley Publishing Group
200 Madison Avenue
New York, N.Y. 10016

# Second Chance at Love

# BEGUILED

## LINDA BARLOW

**SECOND CHANCE AT LOVE
BOOK**

To all the members, past and present, of the Wednesday evening writers' group in Acton, Massachusetts: Debra, Jack, Joe, Karen, Mark, Pam, Paula B., Paula K., Sam, and Steve. Thanks for all your help and encouragement. Without you I never would have come this far!

# CHAPTER
## *One*

SHE RECOGNIZED HIM IMMEDIATELY. Although it had been eleven years since she had last seen him, Viola Bennett felt as if she'd fallen through an emotional time warp as the tall man with curly dark hair strode purposefully toward the platform where she was seated with the panel of experts on detective fiction. He was Stephen Silkwood, the mystery writer, and he was famous, at least among detective fiction buffs. But, staring numbly at him as he directed his steps toward the empty chair beside her, Viola forgot about his novels, which she loathed. All she could think of was the momentous fact that he was the first man she had ever loved.

He was also the first man to break her heart and leave her wretched, and the pain of that experience rushed back with shocking intensity. She thought she'd recovered from that heartache years ago.

She felt like jumping up and fleeing from the auditorium of the small southern Massachusetts women's college where she and her old nemesis were about to meet, but the gritty determination she'd been cultivating for the past two years since her divorce held her firmly in her seat. She couldn't stop herself, however, from shooting an angry glance at George Denton, chairman of the Whittacre College English department, who had assured her that Stephen Silkwood had refused the invitation to participate in tonight's discussion of the modern mystery novel. She had told George that she did not wish to debate with Stephen Silkwood, or even to meet the man.

George had raised a mocking eyebrow at her. "I thought you were gutsier than that, my dear," he'd chided. "Are you afraid he'll want revenge for that nasty review you wrote last month when his latest mystery came out?"

The book review had been nasty; there was no doubt about that. Viola had argued that Stephen's novels pandered excessively to the public's taste for sex and violence. She particularly objected to his suave, tough-guy hero, Maxwell Trencher.

Max Trencher was smooth and elegant on the surface, but underneath he was a macho, sexist brute who shot criminals and slapped women around without a blink of hesitation. Viola's review had suggested that Silkwood ought to depend less on blood and brutality and more on realistic character development and plot. As for his Neanderthal view of women, it should be updated to the twentieth century.

She knew that Stephen had seen her review because she had heard him interviewed on a radio talk show. "V. J. Bennett, whoever he is, is a malicious, illiterate idiot," he had said. "I'll thank him never to read one of my novels again."

He didn't know, of course, that V. J. Bennett was a female assistant professor of English in addition to being a book reviewer, Viola thought mischievously. Still less did he realize that V. J. Bennett was really Viola Quentin, his summer love of eleven years ago, whom he had lied to and abandoned.

Viola pretended to be fiddling with her notes as Stephen Silkwood coiled his long-limbed body into the chair beside her, accidently bumping against one of her slim, stockinged legs. The brief contact electrified her, transmitting a shock that sizzled briefly before hardening into defiance. Why was she hiding in her notes? she asked herself. She recalled George Denton's ironic glance and told herself to stop being such a coward.

Smothering her trepidation, Viola turned to look at the man settling down beside her. His sea-green eyes met and held hers, and once again time was wiped away. The look they exchanged was startlingly intimate, as if for a moment they were in touch with each other's minds. Then something changed, and she saw curiosity in those green depths, and a trace of amusement, perhaps, but not the slightest hint of recognition.

"Am I late?" he asked casually. "I had a bit of car trouble."

He spoke with the impersonality of a stranger. The years that had passed since their final encounter must have erased her image from his mind.

"We were just about to begin," she managed to reply, struggling to keep her voice as neutral as his.

As he turned to glance at the audience and the other panelists, Viola seized the opportunity to examine his features. He was still as attractive as ever. More so, in fact: darkly handsome, with his black hair only faintly touched with gray, the long-lashed green eyes slightly distanced by a pair of wire-rimmed glasses, the angular cheekbones and narrow but sensuous mouth unchanged by time. A tingle went through her as she remembered his mouth . . .

His eyes shifted, and he caught her staring. He smiled as she hurriedly looked away. "Don't be embarrassed. Happens all the time," he said. "You obviously know who I am. Who are you?"

Pinned to her blouse was a tag that bore her name, Professor Bennett. He stared at it for such a long moment that she thought he had identified her as the hostile book reviewer—until she realized that he was focusing on the open neckline of her blouse. She shrugged impatiently, determined not to gratify him with a blush.

"Professor?" he said admiringly. "Well, well. What do you profess?"

"The chairman is attempting to introduce the panel," she returned tightly.

He raised his well-shaped eyebrows at her and turned to pay exaggerated attention to Professor Denton's opening remarks.

He didn't know her! She could hardly believe it. His face and form were branded on her memory for all time, but he had obviously forgotten the many hours they'd spent together back when he had been a protégé of her father, Percy Quentin, also a mystery writer. Viola had been only seventeen, not yet in college. Stephen had been a charming and attractive writer in his mid-twenties who had yet to publish a book.

In those days, Viola recalled, her father and Stephen Silkwood had been as close as father and son. But, because her parents were divorced and Viola was living with her mother in another state, she didn't meet Stephen until the lazy summer before college when she went to Rockport, Massachusetts, to spend her vacation at the seaside with Percy.

Stephen came up several times to visit and talk shop with her father, and he quickly made friends with the cheerful redhead who was his mentor's only daughter. One balmy weekend in late July, he took Viola sailing. Their boat capsized in a gust of wind, throwing them both into the sea. Viola could still remember the rush of emotion she'd felt when Stephen swam up against her slick body in the water, made sure she was all right, fondled her long wet hair, and kissed her eager lips.

She had promptly fallen in love with him with all the excited longing of an inexperienced young woman who had never met such a sexy, sophisticated man. She hadn't found out until later that he was married.

Her father had broken the news to her later that weekend, not long after Stephen left. Percy Quentin must have noticed the way she was moping around, the way she flushed every time Stephen's name was mentioned. "He's got a wife," he'd told her gently. "A lovely, bright young woman. He's an unprincipled rascal. Forget him, child."

Forget him indeed! She'd certainly tried. But she had fallen hard for Stephen, and although he never wrote her any of the letters he'd promised, it had taken a long time for the magic of that warm, hazy weekend to recede into the depths of her mind. And now here he was again, unearthing all those painful memories by the simple fact of his presence.

"What are we supposed to discuss, anyway?" he was asking her under his breath. "Tell me, Professor, so I don't make a total ass of myself."

George Denton was introducing all the panelists and had just mentioned Stephen, to the applause of the students and professors who filled the auditorium. Stephen nodded pleasantly at them while Viola cleared her throat and replied quietly that the panel was going to begin by discussing the diction of suspense in mystery novels of the thirties.

"Good heavens," he muttered. "Wake me up when we get to the symbolism of murder or something equally earthshaking."

"If you don't care for academic discussions, why are you here?" she asked. "I'd heard you weren't coming."

"I wasn't, but my publisher insisted," he returned. "It seems my dynamic presence at such affairs sells books." There was a touch of self-mockery in his voice, which, along with his dark good looks, warmed her slightly toward him. "This sort of thing makes me nervous," he added, half-seriously it seemed.

Once again his deep green eyes flickered over her without a trace of recognition. She felt caught by those eyes, reeled in and drawn to him. They were the same shade as the sea, in whose depths he had first touched her...kissed her...But he didn't remember. A little impatiently, she reminded herself that she didn't wish to remember either.

She was aware that she looked very different now from the seventeen-year-old girl he had known that summer. At twenty-eight, with her tall, slender body tastefully if conservatively clad in a beige silk blouse and a tailored mahogany-colored suit, and with her long, dark red hair gathered into a sleek chignon, she was infinitely more graceful and self-assured than she had been as a teenager.

"Relax," she said archly. "Think of the royalties."

Stephen Silkwood smiled faintly, sipped water from the glass on the table in front of him, and muttered that he wished it were gin.

David Newstead, a colleague of Viola's from the English department, spoke at length about Dashiell Hammett, then asked the audience for questions. Not surprisingly, all of them were directed to Stephen. He spoke well, and amusingly, and he had the grace to attempt to turn the attention of the audience away from himself and back to the panel as a whole.

"I think you ought to ask this lovely lady beside me a question or two," he said pointedly, after his hints on the matter had been disregarded by the mostly young female audience. He glanced once again at Viola's name tag. "Professor, uh, Bennett is undoubtedly an expert on Dashiell Hammett or Agatha Christie or Robert B. Parker or—"

"Or you," David Newstead interrupted shyly. He was sitting on the other side of Viola, and he leaned eagerly across her as he spoke. "She's quite an expert on you, Mr. Silkwood, even if she's not one of your most ardent admirers."

Viola gave David a quelling look. "Sorry," he murmured. "Have I said something wrong?"

Behind his wire-rimmed glasses, Stephen's green eyes narrowed as he stared harder at Viola's name tag. He raised his eyes and looked directly into her face as if they were alone in the room. A palpable shock went through her.

"Not the immortal V. J. Bennett?"

"I'm afraid so," she admitted.

His eyes swept her, impudently this time, as someone from the audience demanded to know why the professor was not one of Stephen's admirers. Viola could feel his gaze resting on the open V of her neckline, modest though it was. "My interest in this discussion has suddenly increased," he whispered. "You'd better have a good answer to that question."

Since she hadn't expected him to show up, Viola had not come prepared to discuss Stephen Silkwood's novels. Besides, although she disliked his work, she felt slightly guilty about having written such a scathing review. His book had come out almost simultaneously with her father's final mystery, *An Intricate Solution,* written just before Percy Quentin's death last summer. Some of the initial reviews had praised Stephen at the expense of her father, and Viola had been furious. Her put-down of Stephen had been her way of leaping to her father's defense.

"Your sadistic hero, Maxwell Trencher, has either shot, raped, or beaten a woman in each of his last three adventures," she said slowly. "Don't you think it's about time he had his consciousness raised, Mr. Silkwood?"

She was speaking at a women's college, and on this subject sympathy ran on her side. Several shouts of approval greeted her statement, increasing her confidence.

"After all," she went on, "books like yours have a certain influence on the people who read them, and it seems almost immoral to me to suggest that it's okay for a man to treat women in the brutal, callous fashion Max Trencher invariably does."

"Maxwell Trencher is a product of my imagination," Stephen responded. "As such he's not subject to any particular system of ethics. I don't suggest that my readers go out and imitate his actions."

"But suppose somebody did? Wouldn't you be morally responsible?"

"If a man murders his brother and marries his sister-in-law on the way home from a matinee performance of *Hamlet,* does that make Shakespeare morally responsible?" he countered.

"Are you comparing yourself with Shakespeare?" Viola asked sweetly.

He grinned. "I'm not that arrogant." He paused a moment, then turned the argument around. "Tell me, Ms. Bennett, by what right do academics like you criticize living writers so harshly? You almost always wait until we're dead before giving us any credit for artistry. Yet without us, where would you people be? You need me, Professor Bennett. You really ought to support my work."

He got a round of applause for this, but something about the way he said, "You need me," and the challenging look in his green eyes when he said it, sent a flash of anger through her. Once, eleven years ago, she had needed him, and he had betrayed her. And although she still felt the pain of that betrayal, he obviously didn't remember ever having met her.

"Plenty of critics support your work," she retorted. "Surely a writer who could create the heartless Maxwell Trencher cannot be affected by the adverse criticism of one insignificant reviewer?"

"You fail to distinguish between the author and the hero," he argued. "For all you know, I might be a shy, insecure individual who reveres women and abhors violence."

But his words were mocking, and the smugness of his tone positively dismissed the possibility that he was either shy or insecure. The way his eyes lingered on her mouth, then on the swell of her softly rounded breasts beneath her suit jacket made it clear that he had no particular reverence for women either. And were it not for his scholarly looking glasses and the fact that he was dressed casually instead of in an expensive three-piece suit, he might have been Maxwell Trencher in the flesh.

"On the other hand," Viola said, smiling archly, "it's also possible that the author and the hero are exactly alike. In which case you couldn't possibly care what some malicious, illiterate idiot has to say about you."

Stephen Silkwood's eyebrows rose extravagantly, but before he could reply to this salvo, George Denton, the moderator, cut in and asked one of the other panelists to say something about Sir Arthur Conan Doyle and his hero, Sherlock Holmes.

"What are you doing after this is over?" Stephen whispered. "The Max in me would like to treat you to a brutal, callous drink."

"You're married," she whispered back.

He looked faintly puzzled. "I'm divorced."

Viola was dismayed at the confused excitement that swept her when she heard this. "There's a reception when this is over," she said, fighting for calm. "You have to be there to sign autographs."

He cursed softly in true Maxwell Trencher style.

The reception in the modern glass and steel art gallery of the fine arts building threatened to go on all night. Stephen Silkwood was mobbed by fans, many of whom had brought copies of his books for him to sign. He was gracious to them all, Viola noted from where she stood conversing with her colleagues and drinking tepid white wine from a plastic cup. He seemed more relaxed now than he had been during the discussion. He laughed easily and flirted with some of the bolder students. He was divorced. She wished he hadn't told her that. She also wished she could force herself to leave, as some of the other panelists already had.

She tried to concentrate on the ramblings of David Newstead, who was making the most of the opportunity to try out his new theory about the decadence of the modern novel. David was a gentle, doe-eyed man who had been persistently inviting Viola to go out with him ever since she had begun teaching at Whittacre the previous fall. She always refused, but he continued to ask her, rather shyly and never with much visible hope that she would accept. Once or twice, feeling lonely, she had nearly said yes, but the fact was that she was not attracted to David. She enjoyed chatting with him at school and occasionally having lunch with him in the college cafeteria, but that was enough.

It had been months since she had last accepted a date. Instead she spent her evenings in the library, doing research and writing articles. In preparation for the time when she would be considered for academic tenure, she was trying to build herself a reputation as a serious scholar. She was also working on a biography of her father.

Although she missed masculine company, she had been much too devastated by the violent breakup of her marriage two years before to rush into any romantic entanglements. That, along with the death of her father last summer, had briefly dampened her usual enthusiasm for life. After beginning the academic year at Whittacre bereaved and alone, she had thrown herself into her work and taught herself to be independent. She felt, at last, that she was succeeding; she had rebuilt her life, and she was relatively happy. The last thing she needed was the disruptive influence of another man in her life.

Stephen Silkwood had worked his way over to the wine table to refill his glass. He smiled at Viola, a good-humored grin that sent an unwanted thrill through her. He was very attractive; there was no denying that. She was immediately struck by the pleasant contrast of his black hair against his fair skin. The gray feathering around his temples confirmed his age to be thirty-seven or -eight, but his overall appearance was as casual and Ivy League as if he had just wandered off the Harvard campus. He was dressed in a brown tweed sports jacket, a rumpled cotton shirt without a tie, blue jeans, and loafers. Standing beside her, he was taller than she had remembered—over six feet. His body was lean and lithe, and he moved with the grace of a dancer. Unlike Max Trencher, Stephen was not brawny, but he conveyed the impression of masculine strength.

"This shouldn't take much longer," he said, gulping down a glass of wine and pouring himself another. "In ten minutes or so you and I can quietly excuse ourselves and make a dash for the door."

"I don't remember accepting your invitation," she returned, a little taken aback. Certainly, she told herself firmly, she had no intention of going anywhere with Stephen Silkwood. Even though she was confident that she'd outgrown her infatuation with him years ago, she remembered her heartache only too well. However charmingly he might smile, in reality Stephen was a coldhearted, manipulative man.

"Don't be difficult," he said with a grin. "I'm your honored guest; it's your duty to entertain me, Professor."

"Let me introduce you to David Newstead. He's a professor of modern literature and a great admirer of yours. He'd be delighted to entertain you," she said mischievously. "David, Mr. Silkwood wants to talk to you about the symbolism of murder."

David Newstead's face lit up, and he held out his hand enthusiastically. Stephen shook it, shooting a nasty look at Viola over David's head. A few minutes later, Viola politely said good night to her department chairman, George Denton, who was a little drunk. He was a gossipy old bachelor, brilliant in his field—eighteenth-century literature—but an unsettling influence at parties. He had a nose for everybody's personal affairs.

"Going home alone again, my dear?" he asked her, his voice fatherly but his mouth set in a leer.

"As usual," she said good-naturedly, sharply conscious of Stephen Silkwood listening from about a yard away.

"A pity. But one of these days, I'm sure, some fine young man will turn up and sweep you off your feet. Then imagine how jealous the rest of us will be."

Viola made a smiling disclaimer and escaped.

Standing beside the plate-glass windows in the corridor, she put on her raincoat and waited for the elevator to take her down to the ground floor. Outside, an early spring thunderstorm was growling. Flashes of lightning revealed the budding branches of the huge oak trees that surrounded the country campus like guardians in the night. The orange-globed lanterns along the brick sidewalk six floors below shone like beacons. Viola buttoned her coat and turned up the collar. It was just beginning to rain.

Overhead, the lights flickered off, then came back on again. The electricity often went off in this building during storms. It was a nuisance.

The elevator doors glided open, and as she stepped in she heard footsteps rapidly crossing the polished tile floor behind her. "Hold it," someone said, and she automatically pushed the open-door button. Stephen Silkwood stepped into the elevator.

"I told them I was going to the men's room," he explained. "Trying to escape me, Professor?"

Viola was aware of a ridiculous blush rising over her features. "It's late," she said briskly. "I have an eight o'clock class tomorrow."

He leaned lazily against the side of the elevator and said, "You can take your finger off the button now, Ms. Bennett. Nobody else is coming. It's just you and me."

Feeling foolish, Viola pushed the ground-floor button, and the elevator started down. They regarded each other. He cocked his head a little to one side, looking puzzled. "You remind me of someone," he ventured. "We haven't met before, have we? I'm sure I'd remember if we had."

A hard knot of anger formed inside her. "No doubt you have an excellent memory—for some things."

"Well, I remember your nasty book review almost word for word. And I particularly remember how it made me squirm when I first read it."

"You don't look like the squirming sort," she commented.

He smiled, his eyes skimming over her body. "On the contrary, I'm very sensitive, Professor, and quite capable of being hurt. I cover up my weakness, however, by striking back. I haven't yet decided how I'm going to take my revenge on you."

"Revenge? That sounds rather melodramatic."

She had no sooner said the word than the soft panel lighting in the elevator went out and the downward motion came to a halt somewhere between the second floor and the third.

"You forget, I write murder mysteries." Stephen's voice was smooth and calm in the blackness. "Melodrama is my forte."

Viola stabbed at the floor buttons in the dark. Nothing happened, but above them there was a click, and an emergency light source came on to dimly illuminate the elevator. Stephen was looking vastly amused.

"Did you do this on purpose?" he taunted. "You'd be surprised to hear to what lengths some people go to spend a few minutes alone with a famous writer."

"You, Mr. Silkwood, have an enormous ego."

"You, Professor, have no sense of humor."

Again she pushed the buttons on the control panel, but the elevator did not respond. She tried the red alarm button, expecting to be jarred by a buzzer or bell, but it, too, was dead. She cursed and banged the panel with the heel of her hand.

"No need to brutalize it," Stephen said cheerfully. "What's the matter—claustrophobia?"

She turned to him, irritated by his unconcern. "You enjoy being trapped in an elevator?"

He raised his eyebrows, seeming to consider. "That depends. I can imagine circumstances in which it could be quite a pleasant experience."

She flushed, aware that he was again taking stock of her body with a kind of predatory ease. His lazy, confident smile reminded her that here was a man who would feel comfortable in almost any situation, whether it be a stuck elevator or an overturned sailboat.

A throb of excitement stirred within her as the memory of that Saturday afternoon all those years ago filled her mind. After embracing her in the water, Stephen had righted the sailboat and steered over to a strip of deserted beach. He had carried her out of the water in his arms, laid her down in the warm sand, and caressed her eager young body into ecstasy.

Standing there in the darkness of the elevator, Viola could almost feel the slant of the hot July sun on her tender skin and hear the lapping of the gentle waves. Stephen's hands had roved ceaselessly over her, sliding from her thick hair to her throat, then to the softness of her breasts beneath her fragile bikini top. Loosening the straps, he had freed her breasts from their confinement, arousing them with his light, fiery touch until her nipples stood in taut points of desire. His fingers proceeded to move lower on her yearning body, down over her tanned, flat stomach, slowly, like a straggler leaving tracks in damp sand, to the warmth of her thighs and the inner edge of her bikini briefs. His kisses became more passionate, his mouth drinking her in. He whispered endearments, love words, promises—words that quickly turned into heated urgings.

She was a virgin, and despite the desire he aroused in her—desire that burned and seared her soul as well as her body—Viola was afraid of the urgency of Stephen's passion. She resisted when he tried to strip off her bikini and take her body to his own there in the warm sand. Excited beyond the point of reason, he had firmly held her down until, overwrought and confused by her own contradictory feelings, she had burst into tears. Stephen had quieted then and become very gentle, comforting her and kissing her tears away.

He had forced their intimacy no further, nor had he complained, as boys her own age were wont to do, that she had led him on. He simply held her close and recited poetry to her while the blue sky wheeled above their heads and the sea gulls called to their mates. He told her that those moments in her arms were timeless and eternal and that he would always treasure them. He hadn't mentioned that he had a wife.

Timeless and eternal indeed, she thought now angrily. He didn't even remember her! For weeks afterward she had loved him with a restless fever, daring any fantasy, even the disturbing one of having an affair with a married man. But she had never heard from him again. So much for his fine promises. Obviously she had been nothing to him but a momentary amusement. If she hadn't been so young and foolish at the time, she told herself now, she would have forgotten him just as efficiently as he had forgotten her.

"Do you have any clever ideas about how to get us out of here?" she asked him, unable to keep the displeasure out of her voice.

He shrugged his angular shoulders. "If it's a power failure, no doubt it will be fixed presently. I suggest we take it easy and wait. Despite our antipathy for each other, it shouldn't be too unbearable." He quirked an eyebrow at her. "After all, bright eyes, you are a beautiful woman, and I am a minor celebrity pursued by detective fiction groupies. A lot of people would just love to be stuck in here with either of us."

He smiled as he spoke, and behind his glasses his eyes looked deep green. His habit of looking directly into her eyes was as forthright as it was challenging. And his body seemed to radiate grace and energy. She caught herself wondering what it would feel like to kiss his sensuous mouth once again.

"If you can stand it, I suppose I can," she said, speaking lightly for the first time and allowing herself to smile. Regardless of his self-satisfied air, Stephen Silkwood had an offhand humor that she couldn't help liking. She got the impression that he didn't take himself too seriously. He certainly wasn't as intense as he had been eleven years ago.

"I'm sorry about the book review," she added spontaneously. "It never occurred to me that you'd take it personally. I needed to get an article published, and because it was so different from what other critics were saying about you, my editor liked it."

"Well, that's refreshingly, honest, at least."

"Besides," she added, "Maxwell Trencher reminds me of my ex-husband, which doesn't dispose me to think kindly of him."

An interested light gleamed in Stephen's eyes. "Did your ex-husband beat you and rape you?" he asked, a bit too casually for Viola's taste. She felt another stab of anger, made all the more bitter by the memory of her last, awful night with Douglas Bennett. Two years, she realized with a shudder, and she wasn't over it yet. Would she never forget the shock of seeing the facade peel off her gentlemanly husband?

"You sound very callous about the idea," she said sharply, her brief spurt of goodwill toward him gone. "Or are you always as unfeeling as your immortal hero?"

He took a step toward her, and she was suddenly conscious of her vulnerability. Intellectually she felt a match for any man, but in terms of physical strength Stephen clearly had the edge. If he chose to force himself on her, there wasn't much she could do to stop him. What was worse, she wasn't even sure she would try. Vulnerable or not, she found the pull between them exciting. There was something about Stephen Silkwood that made her willing, even eager, to take him on.

"Since you persist in confusing me with Max," he said lightly, "perhaps I should just go ahead and be Max." With one hand he reached out and touched a finger to her lips, slowly and delicately tracing the lines of her mouth. There was a hammer blow of sensation in the deepest part of her, and her heart beat heavily. "Max would never forgive me if I didn't at least ravish a kiss out of you," he added.

Before she could protest, his mouth covered hers, sending a jolt of pleasure arcing through her body. For an instant she struggled against him, but his firm, sensitive lips left a burning imprint of memory, exciting all the old feelings she'd thought had been dead for years. His arms came around her yielding form, and he pulled her close against his hard, spare body.

Without hesitation, his hands wandered boldly over the contours of her back, lingering briefly at the belt line of her raincoat, then dipping lower. Her blood pounded in sharp, quick pulses. She could hardly believe what was happening. Held tightly against him, she could feel his excitement, just as she could hear it in his rapid breathing. And from the way she was returning his kiss, her tongue sliding sensuously into his mouth, her fingers tangling in the soft tendrils of hair that curled about his collar, he would know that she was hungry—something she hadn't even known herself.

Was it possible? she wondered dizzily with the small portion of her brain that was still capable of rational thought. Would she really melt for him as easily as she had as a teenager? He didn't even recognize her, damn him! Why couldn't she push him away?

He nudged her back against the wall of the elevator; then, lifting his mouth from hers, he smiled into her eyes and opened the front of her raincoat. She wanted to protest, but she couldn't form the words. Mesmerized, she stared back at him as his hand sought one of her small, firm breasts through the thin fabric of her blouse. Uncontrollably, she arched against him as his maddening fingers traced oval patterns around the spot where her nipple nestled within her lacy bra.

"You intrigue me, Professor," he whispered in a voice made husky by passion. "I felt it as soon as I laid eyes on you."

"Felt what?" she managed to ask as his lips brushed hers lightly, tantalizingly.

But he shook his head and didn't answer, deepening the kiss instead until there was no corner of her warm mouth that his tongue had not sought out and explored. He was thrusting her raincoat farther aside and fingering the buttons of her blouse when she experienced an odd, sinking sensation. She was momentarily disoriented. Then, as her eyes were dazzled by light, she realized that the electricity was back on and the elevator was continuing its descent.

Stephen regretfully took his hand from her breast, saying softly in her ear, "Damn. Just as we were about to get to know each other better. But don't think this means I've forgiven you, Ms. V. J. Bennett. It'll take more than a furtive embrace to get you back into my good graces after that wretched book review."

Viola straightened her raincoat, her heart pounding and her head singing. It was all a joke to him; she realized that from his tone. No doubt he cheerfully molested women in elevators every chance he got. "We know each other quite as well as I could ever wish," she snapped.

The ground floor indicator pinged, and the doors rolled open. She stepped quickly into the hall and made for the glass door that would take her outside into the hard-falling rain.

"Wait," Stephen said, catching her arm just above the elbow. She looked up at him; his eyes were laughing at her. "Don't be angry," he said placatingly. "Come and have a drink with me."

"No. It's late. I'm going home."

"I shouldn't have done that," he persisted, "coming on to you like... I'm really not at all like Maxwell Trencher. Let me prove it to you."

"Please," she said, wrenching her arm free. "I'm tired, and I'd like to go home."

"Give me your number, then. I'll call you."

In a flash she pictured herself waiting day after day by the phone, as she had once waited by the mailbox. She shook her head violently. "No."

Two giggling young women who had been staring at them from in front of the water fountain took this moment to approach.

"Aren't you Mr. Silkwood?" one of them asked while the other blushed and looked foolish. "I love your books. Can we have your autograph? We've got a copy of your latest mystery right here."

Viola shoved open the doors as Stephen turned to oblige the girls. "I'll call you," he repeated ominously as she stepped out into the rain. "Depend on it."

She fled, fighting an absurd urge to cry. "I'll write you. Depend on it." That's what he had said the last time they'd met. It had been her first lesson in the untrustworthiness of men, a lesson later confirmed by her husband's unnerving descent into violence. No, Viola knew better now than to depend on the promise of any man, particularly one who had so thoroughly beguiled her.

# CHAPTER
# *Two*

THE CALL came the following afternoon. Viola was in her office at the college, gathering the books and papers she would need for the weekend, when her extension rang. She answered it absently, her mind still on the student who had left a couple of minutes before. The girl had ostensibly come to talk to Viola about a paper, but it had quickly become apparent that there was something else on her mind. As Viola listened sympathetically, the student had haltingly described the pressure her parents were putting on her to make top grades and get into law school. She felt she was caving in under the stress.

Viola did her best to reassure the girl, remembering the days when she herself had been under similar pressure, first from her father and later from her husband. But there was no longer anyone standing over her like a slave driver, demanding that she fulfill his high expectations of her. She was independent now, with only herself to please. It felt good to be the master of her own fate. Impatiently, she brushed aside the faint suspicion that her fate was a far too lonely one.

"Hello?"

"Hello, Professor," said Stephen Silkwood. "I thought I might be able to reach you there."

His voice instantly set her pulse racing as it called up the disturbing dreams she'd had all night long, inspired, no doubt, by the warmth of Stephen's mouth on hers and the touch of his hands roving her body. "Hello," she returned softly.

"It's Friday," he went on, "so I know you don't have to get up early for a class tomorrow. I thought you might like to take me out to dinner tonight."

"*I* take *you* out to dinner? You must be joking."

"I'm perfectly serious. Considering what your nasty review is costing me in book sales, I figure you owe it to me."

There was a lighthearted quality about his voice that made her smile in spite of herself. "You're a successful novelist," she countered. "Do you have any idea what an assistant professor earns? I can't afford you."

"I thought you were a liberated woman, Ms. Bennett. Well, we'll simply do it the old-fashioned way: I pay for dinner, and you pay me back with your...witty conversation."

It was not, she intuited, what he was really thinking. "Thank you for the charming invitation, but I don't think I can make it."

He must have picked up the faint note of sarcasm in her tone, for he quickly said, "You're still mad at me for what happened in the elevator, aren't you. Listen, I promise to keep old Max firmly under wraps tonight. I don't usually attack perfect strangers; it was a momentary aberration. Full moon or something."

Viola felt herself weakening. The attraction she'd felt eleven years ago was still powerful. She had to admit she was delighted he had kept his promise to call.

But it would be madness to go, she tried to tell herself. He was bound to find out she was Percy Quentin's daughter, and he might even remember something of what had transpired between them on the white sands of the beach that summer. Then they would both be embarrassed and uncomfortable. And, in the end, the same thing would happen: he would say good-bye and go back to wherever he lived and wrote—Cape Cod, she believed—and she would be left with more burning memories to torment her.

"You're hesitating," he noted. "Say yes."

His entreaty sounded so sincere that before she knew what had happened, her resistance crumbled. "Okay," she said.

"Great. Can you be ready by six? Where do you live? Do you like Indian food? My agent in Boston told me about a new Indian place he recommends highly."

He sounded as excited as a schoolboy, and her heart warmed toward him. "I love it," she confessed.

"Professor," he said, "you and I are going to get along just fine."


When she got home, Viola drew a hot bath for herself in the old-fashioned country bathroom of her nineteenth-century farmhouse and soaked deep in a mass of fragrant bubbles in the lion-footed tub. The feel of the silky water against her bare skin relaxed her, and, closing her eyes, she fantasized about making love with Stephen Silkwood.

His tall, rangy body with its hint of wound-up sexual energy stimulated her imagination, as did the thick, curly hair that seemed to invite a woman's caressing fingers. She remembered with a shiver the look in his sea-green eyes when he pinned her against the wall of the elevator, and her body tingled with pleasure at the thought of his lips coaxing hers into surrender, his hands invading all her secret hollows.

There was no denying it: she was still drawn to him. And it was more than just physical. He was clever and amusing, and there was something about the battle of wits that had begun between them on the podium last night that was extremely appealing to her. All in all, she realized, she was anticipating their evening together with unprecedented excitement.

Viola scrubbed herself impatiently when she discovered that the bath was not proving to be as relaxing as she'd hoped. She was beginning to feel as keyed up and nervous as a schoolgirl. After all, it had been two years since her divorce, two years since she'd been involved in anything but the most superficial relationship with a man. It had been a long time since love had been a part of her life.

Stepping out of the tub and toweling her body abrasively, she sternly reminded herself that *love* was a word that didn't exist in Stephen's vocabulary. Nothing could be more foolish than indulging in romantic daydreams about him. If he wanted her at all, it would be for a quick and casual sexual adventure, no more. But she had never been good at casual sex, and despite her new independence, she wasn't sure she could start now.

Wrapping herself in a thick towel, Viola padded out into her eclectically furnished bedroom and sat down on the edge of the huge brass bed to dry her hair. Staring thoughtfully at her reflection in the dressing-table mirror, she wondered why Stephen was bothering to pursue her. Admittedly her deep blue eyes were pretty, but otherwise it was hardly a perfect face. Her nose was uptilted instead of classically straight, and her creamy complexion was splashed here and there by the sprays of tiny freckles so common to redheads. Her mouth was definitely too wide, and there was a determined, almost stubborn, set to her chin. No, it couldn't be her looks, and it certainly wasn't her brains; he'd made it clear that he despised academics.

Neither could he have been swept off his feet by her engaging personality. She had been so full of old memories and resentment that she had barely been polite to him. Had that in itself intrigued him? Was he bored with fawning women—detective fiction groupies, as he'd ungraciously termed them? Did he consider her a challenge?

She frowned at herself, catching her full lower lip in her teeth. Some challenge. One kiss and she'd melted. He probably saw her as easy sexual prey and intended to use her that way tonight. Well, maybe she should go along with it for once. The days were long gone when a woman had to feel ashamed about that kind of thing. He was a very attractive man; maybe she should use him as he undoubtedly intended to use her. He was probably an expert lover. All it would require was not allowing herself to be overwhelmed by his considerable charm; she didn't want to fall for him again. She would have to keep her cool and protect the inner core of herself that longed for more than sex, for a relationship, a partnership. But she ought to be able to manage that, she told herself impatiently. After all, she was no longer seventeen.

She experienced a twinge of doubt, however. There was something deeply unsettling about Stephen Silkwood. She'd sensed it from the moment she'd caught sight of him striding toward her on the podium last night. She feared that if she let him get close to her in any way, all her carefully erected barriers against pain would come crashing down. And that was a risk she simply could not afford to take.

Slipping into a pair of plum-colored briefs and a matching bra, Viola brushed her damp hair vigorously while she went to her closet to consider what to wear. How should she array herself for a cool and casual evening with Stephen Silkwood? The gray wool suit? No, too severe. Her black cocktail dress, on the other hand, was too sexy; spaghetti straps and plunging necklines were definitely out. She finally decided on a green silk dress with pearl buttons down the front. It was the most expensive thing she owned, but despite its fine material, it wasn't overly dressy. With the high neck and the long sleeves, it looked almost prim, except for the way the fabric clung to her slender curves.

She had finished dressing and was just dragging her

hair up into a knot atop her head when the doorbell rang. Damn. He was early.

She opened the front door and found him leaning against the pillar of the porch, grinning. He was dressed as he had been the night before: blue jeans, a tweedy jacket, and, this time, a loosely knotted tie. Despite the lazy masculinity of his hard, lanky body, there was something endearingly rumpled about him. She half expected to see ink smudges on his finger and thumb.

"Nice dress," he said, his eyes sweeping impudently from her soft high breasts to her slender waist and down her long legs before coming back to her face.

"You're early," she returned, impatient with the blush she felt rising over her cheeks. "I'm not quite ready."

"You should be flattered; obviously I'm overeager," he said with the same appealing touch of self-mockery she had noted during the panel discussion. "May I come in?"

"Of course." She opened the storm door.

"Do you own this house?" he asked, following her into the living room and looking around at the antique furniture, the eighteenth-century reproductions on the walls, and the ornately carved bookcases overflowing with hardback volumes.

"No. I'm renting it from a colleague who's on sabbatical this year. I couldn't afford a place like this."

"No, I suppose not. Not on your salary," he said, obviously teasing her about her earlier remark. He strolled over to the baby grand piano in the corner and touched a few keys.

"Do you play?" she asked, trying to remember.

"Not seriously. Do you?"

She shrugged. "A little. I don't practice enough. Would you like a drink while I finish dressing? The bar's over there on the sideboard. There's ice in the bucket."

"You look dressed to me. What else are you going to put on—armor?"

She laughed spontaneously. "Will I need it?" she demanded, falling into the same light, bantering tone he employed so adeptly.

He moved a couple of paces toward her, his eyebrows pleasantly quirked. "That depends on you, Professor. You were extremely combative last night, weren't you? Verbally, at least," he added significantly, and she knew he was remembering her brief physical surrender in the elevator.

"With the cutthroat competition in my profession, a certain amount of combativeness is required," she said, deliberately pretending to misunderstand him. "I'm sorry if it disturbed you to match wits with a woman."

"It didn't disturb me in the least," he responded complacently. "Would you like a drink, too?"

"No, thanks. You have one. I have to go fix my hair."

Her bedroom was on the first floor at the end of the back hall. When she reached it she discovered that Stephen was ambling after her, drink in hand, surveying with interest the intricate labyrinths of the old farmhouse. He hesitated for only an instant on the threshold before joining her in the bedroom. She tried to ignore the tightening deep down inside her that his presence inspired.

"You don't sleep upstairs?" he asked casually.

"I like the fireplace," she explained. The room was equipped with a huge brick hearth. "This used to be the kitchen, years ago. Its other advantage is that it gets the afternoon sun."

There was no fire on the hearth now, although one was burning in the living room. Viola had certainly not planned on entertaining Stephen in her bedroom.

With affected ease, she sat down in front of the walnut dressing table and caught up the few strands of long, thick hair that were not yet secured atop her head. Stephen strolled around, inspecting the room as if he were a potential house-buyer. He came to a stop at the frame of her old-fashioned bed.

"A brass bed," he observed, fingering a rail. His eyes caught hers in the mirror. "What a good idea. It's just what Max needs in his apartment. He's keen on binding his women to the bed frame so he can ravish them at leisure." He smiled, his green eyes once again assessing her body. "Very exciting. Ever tried it?"

Viola struggled to keep her composure, even though her blood was streaming like quicksilver through her veins. His bold eyes and the subtle suggestiveness of his husky voice provoked a far stronger response than she cared to admit. Everything about him inspired visions of ecstatic lovemaking.

"Good old Max," she said with a casualness she was not feeling. "I suppose you share his bizarre sexual preferences?"

He laughed. "Has anybody ever told you you have a very acid tongue?"

"A few."

Leaning back against the head of the bed with his arms folded against his chest, he considered her in the mirror. "It must be the hair. Fiery hair, fiery nature."

Viola was having trouble arranging said fiery hair. She was determined not to be overwhelmed by Stephen's disturbing presence in her bedroom, but her fingers were unsteady, and strands of hair kept escaping.

"No," he said, as if he suddenly realized what she was doing. He stepped up behind her, pushed her hands away, and began tearing the pins out of her hair. The touch of his fingers against her scalp sent shivers rippling through her.

"Lord," he muttered as the flaming masses fell about her shoulders. "Your hair is beautiful. Why do you bind it up in that schoolmarmish fashion? With your tresses loose, my dear, you look like an entirely different person."

Staring dazedly at herself in the mirror, Viola's heart caught in her throat. She looked different, all right. She looked almost the way she had at seventeen.

Stephen made a low sound in his throat. He was standing over her now, his graceful, long-fingered hands falling lightly on her shoulders as he stared at her reflection. A strange expression had come over his face, and a frown flickered at the corners of his narrow mouth.

"Professor," he said slowly. "Do you realize that I don't even know your first name? What does the *V* stand for?"

"Viola," she answered faintly. "My name is Viola."

"I once knew a girl with that name." His eyes were locked with hers.

She couldn't speak.

His mouth hardened, as did his eyes. "Her father was my enemy, and she herself was a bitch," he added brutally.

He must have felt the shock that shuddered through her, for his hands tightened on her shoulders. "Let me go," she said furiously, but he paid no attention. His eyes had caught sight of the picture of her father, which was propped up on one side of her dressing table. She had forgotten it was there.

"I don't believe it," he said. His voice sounded harshly metallic, and the light reflecting from the table lamp glanced oddly off his glasses, making his eyes look as if they were emitting sparks. "You're Percy Quentin's daughter."

"I've been trying to think of a way to tell you," she replied. "Naturally you didn't remember me," she added sarcastically.

"But you knew who I was," he snapped, his mouth twisting in anger. "You accepted my invitation, knowing all along that I never would have issued it if I'd realized your identity."

Viola flushed with a combination of embarrassment and rage. She had known it would be awkward, but somehow she hadn't expected so violent a reaction on his part. He was glaring at her as if she were the daughter of the devil himself. She tired, unsuccessfully, to twist out of his hold. His fingers bit into her shoulders.

"You pressed me, Stephen," she pointed out. "I tried to discourage you. It serves you right for being so determined to sweep me off my feet. Anyway, what do you have against my father?" she asked bitterly as the pain of Percy Quentin's slow death welled up in her. "He helped you when you were young and unknown. He took an interest in your writing long before any agent or publisher would give you the time of day. You've got a nerve to describe him as your enemy."

"And to describe you as a bitch?" he said softly. One of his hands slid from her shoulder to her throat, where her pulse was beating hard. "I thought when I kissed you in the elevator that your body was no stranger to me," he went on. "I felt it, in fact, as soon as I sat down beside you for that inane panel discussion. It's a bit unusual for me to want a woman so intensely within moments of meeting her. But it was an awakening of old feelings, not the creation of new ones."

His voice was caressing and harsh at the same time, and Viola's senses were reeling. "I don't care to awaken any old feelings, thank you," she managed to say. "Let go of me."

He shook his head. "There's a piece of unfinished business between us, Viola." He inclined his head in the direction of her bed. "And we just happen to be in the perfect place to finish it."

He remembered the beach, she realized. He remembered everything.

His fingertips burned through the fragile silk of her dress as they moved over her collarbone to the primly fastened neckline. He unbuttoned the top button.

She tried not to panic at the rush of anticipation she experienced. Her body, once again, was reacting to him; inside her, her bones had turned to water. She couldn't understand it. She hated aggressive, domineering men.

"You must be out of your mind," she said desperately. "Take your hands off me."

He paid no attention, opening the next two buttons and sliding his warm hand in against her bare skin. He brushed one of her tingling nipples with his fingertips, causing her to arch away from the touch in a vain effort to escape his exciting ministrations. He moved in closer behind her, effectively trapping her between the dressing table and his hard body. "Better sit still," he said warningly. "Like our friend Max, I'm dangerous when I'm angry."

An alarm flashed in Viola's brain as it occurred to her that in admitting Maxwell Trencher's creator to her isolated country home, she had placed herself in the hands of a man much stronger than she, a man who apparently held a grudge against her father, a man who had already demonstrated his sexual aggressiveness by forcing an embrace on her in an elevator. What if he was violent? How did she know he wasn't? How well had she really known him, after all, eleven years ago? Max Trencher was a woman-hater, and Stephen had made no apologies for Max last night at the college. For all she knew to the contrary, Stephen could be just as brutal as Douglas had turned out to be, or even worse.

"I won't be threatened," she said, more calmly than she felt. "I demand that you get out of my bedroom immediately. Maybe your macho act impresses some women, but I can forgo the pleasure, thank you."

Bracing himself against her dressing-table stool and holding her tightly against his body with one arm around her waist, he threaded a series of short, quick kisses along her hairline from her temple to her ear. His touch was gentle, contradicting his ruthlessness of a moment before. When he pressed his mouth to the hollow at the base of her throat, she felt a primitive pulse of arousal.

In the silvery light of the mirror, she could see his fingers, dark and masculine against her white skin, as they continued to undo her pearl buttons until the green silk of her dress hung open from her collar to her waist.

"I don't believe this," she whispered as he unfastened the front hook of her bra and folded the silky material away from the veined marble of her breasts. "If you think you can waltz back into my life and pick up where we left off, you're mistaken."

"You're very calm," he responded, meeting her smoky blue eyes in the mirror. His fingertips touched the scampering pulse in her throat, and his mouth turned up in a sardonic smile. Scooping both his palms under her breasts, he rubbed his thumbs back and forth over their rosy tips. "Doesn't it excite you to see how sexy you are?" he asked her, kissing her fiery hair. "It excites me, Viola," he added, his voice low and husky. Wrapping a long lock of her hair around one of his wrists, he pulled it taut until she felt a half-painful, half-erotic tug on her scalp. In response, all her nerves tingled and sparked with hot currents of inflamed desire.

With a determined effort of will, she pressed her hands on the edge of the dressing table for leverage and tried to stand up. Somewhat to her surprise, his arms fell away and he didn't try to stop her. They stood for a moment facing each other, close enough to embrace but not quite touching. Viola was acutely conscious of the brass bed less than a yard away, and of the way his sea-green eyes, darkened by passion, were silently inviting her to lie down with him there.

Drawing a deep, steadying breath, she turned and walked out of the room. At the threshold of the living room she stopped and switched on the overhead light, noticing, as she tried to refasten her clothes, that her hands were trembling. Losing patience with the tiny pearl buttons, she crossed over to the fireplace, where the red coals from the afternoon fire were still glowing, and added several sticks of wood.

As the fire blazed up, there was a sound behind her. Stephen entered the room and snapped the light off again, leaving them in semidarkness. His shadow leaped huge against the wall as he came toward her, shedding his jacket and taking off his glasses, which dropped with a definitive click on the surface of a small marble-topped table.

He did not speak; he simply advanced on her, his determined eyes caressing her tense body. She waited, her cheeks hot from the fire but the rest of her glowing from the blaze he had kindled within. When he reached her, she pressed her hands ineffectually against his shoulders as he locked her in a fierce embrace.

Her "No, Stephen...please..." was lost against his mouth as it closed upon hers, and her struggles, too, were quickly eclipsed by the heart-stopping pressure of his sensitive lips against hers. There was no fighting him. How could there be when to break from him would mean withstanding a thundering force that seemed to spring from the deepest well of her being? The ache of passion erupted in her, making her as soft and unresisting as finger-warmed clay against his demanding body. When he rubbed his thumb the length of her spine, up and down, several times, she shivered against him and opened her mouth for his tongue.

"Mmm," he murmured, lifting his lips for an instant, "I think you like my macho act after all, my flaming, red-haired witch."

Her eyes looked into his, and she perceived, through all his outrageous male aggressiveness, the hints of light-hearted laughter that made his macho act precisely that: a performance designed instinctively to give her pleasure. Not a calculated performance, she thought dazedly, but rather a sort of shared fantasy...as if he knew her secret dreams and imaginings and had become one with them, as he would make her one with his own.

It was an odd, surrealistic impression, and it faded immediately as he bent his head again. Defying the inevitable, she turned her face away so that his lips met the curtain of her hair, which he nuzzled briefly before clamping one hand firmly against her scalp and forcing her mouth back to his. His other hand moved purposefully down her back, stroking her hips through the thin silk of her dress until she arched herself against him.

"Kiss me, Viola," he urged, his voice low-timbred with desire. His warm breath against her lips acted like a drug, and this time she obeyed.

Her qualms vanished under the pressure of her desire, and as her fire spread, she matched his advances with her own, sliding her tongue against his, running her fingers over the smooth sinews of his back in quest of deeper pleasure. His body was more muscular than she had realized; he was slim like a runner, but he had the strength and coordination of a wrestler. Her fingertips caressed the ridges of his ears and wandered eagerly down over the nape of his neck. She liked the feel of his strong-boned shoulders beneath her palms; she liked the fresh, masculine scent of him and the way the pulse in his throat beat fast and raggedly, a sign of his intense arousal.

For several moments it was she who controlled the kiss, darting her tongue against his and deepening her penetration of his warm mouth while he remained passive before her tender assault. Then he swept her body very thoroughly with his hands, swung her up into his arms, and carried her over to the plump-cushioned crimson sofa in front of the fire. She kicked off her shoes on the way.

He laid her down on her back, then stepped away. She caught her bottom lip in her teeth in a brief, uncertain gesture as he removed his tie and tossed it across the nearest chair. This was happening too fast . . . and it had begun in anger . . . they hadn't settled anything . . . he had called her a bitch. She closed her eyes, and almost instantly she heard his voice probing her from where he stood, loosening the collar of his shirt.

"Viola?"

Her eyes snapped open, and she was riveted by the smudge of curly hair beneath the open collar at his throat. Oh Lord, he was so exactly the man of her dreams: tall, slim-built but powerful, and much sexier than any man had the right to be, with those lively, expressive eyes and that wicked smile. His masculinity was calling out to the woman in her, summoning her with a force no man had ever exerted upon her before—except one, eleven years ago . . .

"You okay?" he asked her, but the question, she knew, meant more than that.

He wanted to make love to her, and the haze of desire had settled so thickly over her mental processes that she couldn't think of a single reason to object. Worse, she didn't want to be the passive, easily led partner of that afternoon on the beach; she wanted to unchain her responses and meet him equally, with all the uninhibited joy of a passion she reserved for him alone. He might not know it, but he was special to her. Even if she never saw him after tonight, this was a moment to seize and to treasure.

She met his questioning eyes in silent acquiescence. As his fingers went once again to his shirt buttons, Viola caught his other hand and drew him down until he was kneeling on the thick carpet beside the sofa. "Let me," she whispered, raising her hands to his shirtfront.

Slowly she unbuttoned the garment, revealing a little more of his thick chest hair with each button she freed. As he shrugged out of the shirt, she thrilled to the erotic memory of his bare, suntanned body coming down on hers in the sand. Time seemed to evaporate. She felt that she knew him intimately and loved him, and that his body was the only one she ever wanted to take to her own. She had lost him then, but now, once again, he was hers.

He began to ease her back on the sofa, but she surprised him by sliding down to the rug with him and pushing him firmly down on his back. His green eyes laughed at her again as he complied, and he whispered mischievously, "Who, my dear, is seducing whom?"

"Are you objecting?"

"Do I look as if I'm objecting? I like masterful women."

Her eyes were heavy-lidded with desire as she bent over him and touched her lips to his. "I don't believe you for a moment," she returned. "You like nothing better than to run the entire show. But this time, I'm afraid, you're going to get more than you bargained for, Max."

He grinned and pulled her down onto him. "Yeah?" he said delightedly. "Sexy lady. Show me."

# CHAPTER
## *Three*

VIOLA KNEW DIMLY that she would be appalled at herself later for her uncharacteristic surrender to passion there on the hearth rug with the man who had once broken her heart. But the sultry darkness of the room, combined with the warm glow of the fire, which cast strange shadows on their bodies, lent a sense of mystical enchantment to their encounter. Lost in the sensual witchery of the moment, she could think of nothing more than her breathless need to know the subtle pleasures that his sea-green eyes had been promising from the moment they'd first locked with hers.

Leaning over him so that her hair drifted over his naked shoulders, Viola began to explore the warm, furred flesh before her, reveling in the way he responded to each tantalizing touch of her fingers. She trailed her hands over the angular planes of his handsome face, brushing his lips lightly and feeling her fingers sucked and nipped gently in response. She kissed the hollow above his collarbone, then, locating one of his male nipples through the thick, wiry hair, she kissed her way to it and curled her tongue around it until it hardened. Stephen made a low sound, and his body moved convulsively. His hands stopped wandering through her hair to pull her face harder against his naked chest.

"You've changed, Viola," he murmured. "You used to be so timid."

She raised her head to meet his eyes. "I was seventeen. You were the first man I'd ever—" *Loved,* she had been about to say. "Experimented with," she finished.

Something shifted in his expression, and in the mood between them as well. "Is that what it was? An experiment?"

She didn't want to admit the hurt she had suffered. He hadn't cared about it then, and he would probably feel nothing but amusement to hear about it now. "Sex is experimental for most people at that age," she said lightly.

"And what is it now, may I ask? Now that you're obviously well past the experimental stage?"

"What's the matter?" she teased him. "Are you afraid I'll use you only to gratify my raging lust?"

He jerked her down on top of him, and she gasped at the first contact of her soft breasts with his bare chest. His long legs wrapped around her, and in the cradle of his hips she could feel the thrust of his manhood against her. "You'll gratify mine, too, while you're at it," he said roughly. "Your little experiment didn't take you that far eleven years ago, as I recall."

He was angry, she realized, looking in vain for the usual hint of humor around his eyes. He didn't like the idea of being used. She felt a pulse of vengeful satisfaction. It served him right for what he had done to her that summer.

But her taste of victory was fleeting. Stephen rolled over unexpectedly, taking her with him and pinning her beneath his body. "That's better," he rasped as his hands began to move over her with cool, masculine assurance. "As you so perceptively put it, I like to run the entire show." One hard, jeaned thigh slid between her legs, parting them intimately, while his fingers captured a nipple and flicked it to an achingly alive point. She moaned, half in excitement, half in discomfort, for he was not gentle. She could feel the thrust of his body against hers, and the buckle of his belt was chafing the tender flesh of her belly.

"You're crushing me," she protested, finding no give in the hardwood floor beneath the carpet.

He paused in nibbling the lobe of her ear long enough to taunt, "What's the matter—getting more than you bargained for?"

She didn't like the mood that had somehow been created, and she began to struggle against him. He raised himself on his elbows, keeping her legs firmly trapped under his, and slanted a tight, uncompromising glance into her eyes. "An experiment," he said, as if he were still mulling over her words of a few minutes ago. "Funny. I've always thought of it as more in the nature of a trick."

Freeing one hand, she thrust her now wild hair out of her eyes. "What exactly do you mean?"

His lips curled sardonically. "You know perfectly well what I mean," he said. He ran his tongue over her lips, probing the corners of her mouth until she shivered with waves of tingling desire. He obviously felt her response and smiled like a hunter who knows he's run his prey to ground. "What a lot you've got to answer for, Professor." His tongue invaded her, pushing past her teeth to taste the warm honey of her breath before he spoke again. "I never thought revenge could be so sweet."

She twisted her face away. "Damn you!" she cried with anger that surprised them both. "I want to know what you mean, Stephen. What trick? I didn't trick you in any way, and it's you, not me, who has a lot to answer for!"

"We'll discuss it later," he said calmly, hooking his fingers in her hair and repositioning her face where he could get at her. He kissed her eyelashes, her nose, her chin, and, once again, her mouth. "Relax," he soothed, "it's ancient history. Who cares? You're stunning, darling. I want you. Let's get rid of the rest of our clothes and do this properly."

But reality had reentered her world, and relaxing was impossible. She struggled to roll out from under him, but he shifted his weight relentlessly and did not permit it.

"I must be crazy," she said, pushing futilely against his broad shoulders. A thread of fear snaked along her nerves as she remembered the brutal truth of what a determined, angry male could do to a woman who defied him. Maxwell Trencher, she thought. Douglas. "Let me up, Stephen," she insisted, her voice rising slightly in pitch as anxiety tightened around her lungs.

"Oh, no, darling, I'm afraid you're committed now. You want me just as much as I want you, so don't pretend to deny it."

He caught her thrashing arms and pinned them to the carpet. She arched against his strength but could not free herself. Her breath rasped in her throat as the threads of panic multiplied. "Let me go," she cried, closing her eyes to shut out the green stab of his angry glare. "I've changed my mind, Stephen."

"It's too late to change your mind. You're not a child anymore, Viola, and I'm damned if I'll let you play childish games with me!"

"I'm not playing a game, and I'll change my mind any time I damn well please! This is the twentieth century, and women no longer have to endure the old frustrated-male guilt trip. Get off me, damn you. I don't owe you any explanations."

He abruptly changed tactics, kissing her eyelids gently and murmuring, "Don't fight me, sweetheart. You're so tense and stiff all of a sudden, but you were soft and yielding a few minutes ago. I'm not going to hurt you. Why are you afraid of me?"

"I'm not afraid of you!" she snapped.

"You're trembling."

"In case you hadn't noticed, you've got me pinned to the floor!"

"Some women might find that exciting," he returned, lifting his eyebrows in imitation of a rakish leer. "Are you sure you're not one of them?"

Viola was about to scream abuse at him, but something in his expression stopped her. His eyes were looking into her soul, and it was as if he somehow knew that she frequently had romantic fantasies about being swept off into the arms of an irresistible black-haired pirate, who would make passionate love to her despite her unconvincing protests.

Before she could banish the image, Stephen seized the moment and bent his head to kiss her again. His warm lips teased and molded hers, coaxing the embers of her passion to flame again. She twisted her wrists against the fingers that held them, but he didn't release her. To her amazement, the constriction at her wrists sent a thrill of pleasure through her. He was right, she realized dazedly; there was something secretly exciting about the idea of submitting to his sexy, masculine domination.

He must have recognized her near surrender, for he lifted his lips long enough to say, "I'm going to let you go long enough to finish undressing, sweetheart. Then I'm going to love you long and hard and thoroughly, until you cry aloud for mercy."

She shook her head, trying to ignore the throbs of desire reverberating through her body at the sound of his blatantly sensual threats. "No," she whispered, "no, please, I'm not ready for this. I need time. I never should have agreed to go out with you, much less let you into my house. It was a mistake. It was all silly, nostalgic weakness on my part. I don't know how I could have been so foolish."

"Viola, for heaven's sake!" His voice was impatient now.

"Let me up, Stephen. I mean it," she insisted just as impatiently. His arousal was obvious, and the more she squirmed against him, the more he pressed his lower body against her. "Stop it!" she cried. "You infuriate me, acting so aggressive and domineering. I hate that! Haven't you ever been refused before? Do you imagine you're so incredibly irresistible? What are you going to do if I continue to struggle—rape me?"

There was a short, electric silence. Then he slowly said, "No, I'm not going to rape you."

His hands released her wrists, and he pushed himself up and off her quivering body. She felt a draft from the cool room as soon as he moved. The fire on the hearth had died down to a few glowing coals.

He lay beside her with his hands clenched behind his head, remaining very still for several minutes, obviously trying to control his frustration. The task was not any easier for her; a part of her wanted to cry at the thought of what she was losing by being so stubborn.

"I would never descend to physical violence," Stephen went on, pushing himself up on one elbow to glare at her. "You see, my love, I am not Max. Max wouldn't have stopped."

She didn't want to be called *my love*—not in that sarcastic manner. "Three cheers for you," she said furiously.

"What I will do, I suppose, is take out my anger in the press, exactly as I'd planned. I'll finish my article and send it out. That'll fix you, darling—you *and* your father."

She was confused by the sudden shift back to the subject of her father. "I don't know what you mean," she said. "I never understood what happened between you and my father. One day you were as close as father and son, and the next you weren't speaking to each other. But whatever it was, it certainly had nothing to do with me."

His fingers reached out and caressed a nipple with a pressure that made her catch her breath. "Don't lie to me, Viola. You played with me very cleverly that day on the beach, particularly considering your youth. What were you, sixteen going on forty?"

"I was seventeen and in love with you!"

"In love? Come now, there's not a Quentin on the face of the earth who knows what the word means!"

"How dare you say that? I fell for you as only an idiotic seventeen-year-old could. I listened to your empty professions, believing them all, and I waited for your letters for weeks afterward, even though I knew by then that you were married. You used me, Stephen Silkwood, to amuse yourself on a hot summer afternoon when you had nothing better to do. You've got some nerve to act as if it were my fault!"

His expression had altered slightly. "I wrote to you, Viola. Are you actually trying to tell me that you never received my letters?"

"Of course I never received your nonexistent letters, and I'm not going to listen to any lies about them now!"

His eyes looked dark and shadowed. She noticed the crinkly lines around them, faint signs of his aging. They hadn't been so prominent before. "I'm not lying to you," he said slowly. "I wrote to you twice. Percy told me that you read my letters aloud to him and laughed. He even quoted a few passages."

"What?" she whispered, in shock.

"And I wasn't married at the time. I'd been separated from my wife for some time, and my divorce became final that summer, shortly before I met you. Did Percy tell you I was still married?"

She nodded unwillingly. Her father's words were engraved on her heart: "He's got a wife . . . lovely young woman . . . unprincipled rascal . . . forget him."

"Of course," said Stephen bitterly. "I should have guessed." He sat up and pulled his shirt back on, looking weary and disgusted. "He lied to you, Viola. He knew better than anyone else that my marriage was over." He scowled. "Good old Percy. Even from the grave he plagues me."

The silence was broken only by the shifting coals of the dying fire. Viola stared at Stephen, who in turn was staring at his clenched fists. After a few moments he glanced at her face, and then down at her breasts, which were still visible beneath the open buttons of her dress. His look was like a touch, and her body stirred again for him. But the glow of passion had faded from his eyes, and the driving tension in his body had slackened. "Where did I leave my drink?" he asked. He got up and walked over to the bar to pour himself another.

"Stephen, I don't understand. Are you saying that my father deliberately deceived me about you? That he intercepted your letters? I can't believe that. He wouldn't do such a thing. Not my father. It can't be true."

"You didn't know him very well, did you?" he said heavily. "Your own father, and you didn't know what he was like."

The uncertainty she was feeling hardened into anger. "I knew him better than anyone!" she declared. "After his stroke I lived with him and nursed him through all those horrible months until he died. He had nobody else then, except me."

Stephen laughed harshly. "Nobody else could stand him."

She sat up, hugging her knees. "Why do you hate him so much?" she demanded.

"Believe me, you don't really want to know."

"But I do. I'm writing his biography. I want to know everything about him."

He raised his eyebrows in mockery. "His biography! The ultimate paean of praise, no doubt. It will hardly be unbiased, will it, darling? No more objective, I'll bet, than V. J. Bennett's assessment of my talents. You put me down in that review because you didn't think I measured up to Percy's standards, didn't you? You resented me because I turned to writing a different kind of book."

"If you're still angry about my review . . ." she began.

He stalked back to her, standing over her with his fists on his slim hips and his legs braced slightly apart in as aggressive a posture as she could imagine outside a swashbuckler movie. She pushed herself up to sit rather primly on the sofa, her hands clutching nervously at the open buttons of her dress.

"Forget the review!" he half shouted at her. "It's not important. All that's important, Viola Quentin, is the interesting question of whether or not you're lying to me about what really happened that weekend."

His anger, which was still incomprehensible to her, made her reckless. "And what if I am?" she demanded. "What if I'm exactly the liar you think I am? Will that break your heart, Stephen? Will you go home and mourn for the sweet, adoring, sexually cooperative Viola-who-might-have-been?"

He stepped closer to her and put a restraining hand on the fingers that were furiously buttoning her dress. Their eyes met, and his changed in a way she couldn't fathom. His hand fell back to his side.

"No," he said, more to himself than to her. "I may be lustful and undisciplined, but I'm damned if I'll stay here tonight and let you tear me apart all over again."

His words struck her as odd, as if they should be coming from her side of the battle lines, not from his. In what way had she ever torn him apart? He was the one who had hurt her.

"Dammit, Stephen, what have I done? Why do you hate me? Why do you hate my father?" She held his glance, which was burning green fire. "You have to tell me. You owe me an explanation."

"You'll get one soon enough, when my article comes out."

*"What* article?"

"What article do you think?" he said nastily. "Don't sit there pretending to be innocent. Did you seriously imagine I'd sit back and do nothing? This is only the beginning, I assure you. I'm also planning to hit you with a lawsuit."

"Stephen," she said helplessly, "explain."

"Your precious father was a literary cheat, Viola. A thief. One of his novels was plagiarized from an early manuscript of mine. I can't believe you don't already know all about it."

The shocks were coming too fast for her to absorb. She curled up on the edge of the sofa, staring wordlessly at his dark curly hair and his long lashes flickering over his angry green eyes.

"Nothing to say for a change? No witty retort?" Once again he touched her. The clever, long-fingered hands she was beginning to know moved lightly over her flaming crown of hair, wrapped themselves in her tresses, and jerked her head back, forcing her to look up into his face. "If I were Max now, darling, I'd drag you back into the bedroom, throw you down across that inviting bed of yours, and brutalize you until I felt a little better."

"Then you'd be lashing out at someone who's never harmed you, Stephen, except in writing that review," she got out. "I can't answer for my father. If he injured you, I'd like to hear the details. I would like you to explain your very serious accusations."

She spoke coolly, but she was shaking under his hands. He stared down at her for a moment, looking uncertain. Then his mouth hardened.

"Someone like you doesn't deserve an explanation," he said. With that he turned and slammed out of the living room and out of the house.

# CHAPTER
## *Four*

WHEN VIOLA HEARD the bang of her front door and the roar of Stephen's car, the sounds released her own anger. With trembling fingers she picked up his empty Scotch glass from the coffee table and flung it at the wall. It shattered and sent silver shards of glass clinking all over the hardwood floor. She jumped up and hurried over to the window in time to see the fading red gleam of his taillights as he pulled out of her long driveway into the street, and to hear the faint sound of tires screeching as he violently accelerated.

Collapsing in a chair by the window, Viola tried to gather her wits. Her body still ached with unrelieved desire. Dear heaven, how he had touched her! It was going to be just like before, she realized. Worse. For how many weeks would she remember his caresses this time, lying alone in her bed feverishly reliving each moment? For how long would she go over in her mind everything that had been said between them, trying to make sense of his bitter accusations?

She had certainly never lied to him, or tricked him. He had a nerve to suggest that she had! As for what Stephen had said about her father, it was all a pack of lies. Her father must have hurt Stephen somehow, and this was Stephen's way of retaliating. Clearly he'd been carrying a grudge for years.

She knew that Stephen's association with her father had ended abruptly, but she had never known why. She'd fleetingly wondered if it had had something to do with her, since the breach had occurred that same summer, shortly after her abortive romance with Stephen. Had Stephen really written to her? Had her father really intercepted his letters? For heaven's sake, why?

She wandered into her study and sat down at her desk in front of her notes on her father's life and reviews of his works, the material out of which she intended to construct a biography. Another picture of her father was propped up on the desk, taken several years before his devastating stroke. His face was thin and ascetic-looking, his eyes small and round and distant.

"You didn't know him very well," Stephen had said. Could there be truth to this? She tried to recall when her father had ever spoken to her of anything personal—his hopes, his fears, his desires. Very rarely. Yet she had felt close to him. His death still caused a pain in her that seemed sometimes as if it would never dissipate.

She had loved him. And she knew he had loved her, too, even if he'd found it difficult to say so. She'd been able to feel the love Percy had so rarely expressed, the love that had all gone to her after his wife—her mother—deserted him.

Viola's parents had been divorced when she was thirteen. Although she had lived mostly with her mother, Viola had never completely forgiven Martha Quentin for leaving her husband. "He hurt me deeply" was all her mother would say in her own defense. But she had been the one who had broken the marriage and, after less than

a year, married another man. Percy had lived alone for
the rest of his life. It had been he, surely, who had
suffered the most.

But now, along came Stephen Silkwood, also claiming to have been hurt somehow by her father. There was
more to it than his accusation of plagiarism, she intuited.
There was something else, she was certain, that he hadn't
told her. The plagiarism charge, after all, was ridiculous.
Her father was a highly original, creative writer, and
unsuccessful young writers—which Stephen had been at
the time in question—were always claiming to have had
their ideas lifted. Stephen had a volatile temper; he and
Percy had probably fought over something, and Stephen
had latched on to the plagiarism idea as an excuse for
his anger. His style and Percy's were entirely different.
No, it was utterly impossible.

This conclusion relieved her somewhat. She had been
very disturbed, she realized, by Stephen's accusations.
As her father's literary biographer and biggest fan, she
was extremely annoyed by any slight to his professional
reputation. And she was ready to do battle, if necessary,
to defend him. Her father had been a great writer, and
Stephen Silkwood was a popular hack in comparison.
He was probably just jealous because he knew he'd never
measure up to Percy.

The telephone rang. Viola jumped as if she'd been
struck. It's Stephen, she thought. He's sorry. He's coming back. "Hello?"

"Uh, Viola?"

"Yes?"

"It's David Newstead."

Damn, she said to herself.

"Uh, from school," he added when she didn't speak,
as if he didn't expect her to remember him.

"Hello, David. How are you?" she managed, trying
to sound friendly. There was no reason to be rude to him
just because she hated Stephen Silkwood.

"I'm fine. The reason I'm calling is—that is, I know
you're probably busy and all—but there's a concert to-

night in the arts center, and they're playing Mozart and Vivaldi. You told me once that you loved Mozart, so I was wondering if you'd like to go."

He sounded so awkward and diffident, nothing like Stephen at all. But underneath his shyness he was a tactful, reliable man, Viola knew.

"I'm sorry to call so late," he added before she could get a word in. "You're probably eating dinner or something. I just found out about the concert half an hour ago, and I thought it would be nice not to have to go alone. But if you're busy—"

"I'm not busy," she interrupted impulsively. "I'd be glad to go with you, David. What time does it start?"

"At eight. Does that give you time to get ready?" he asked anxiously.

She glanced down at her green silk dress with an ironic smile. "I can be ready in five minutes," she told him, and she gave him directions to her house.

Viola had a more pleasant time with David that evening than she had expected. He was hardly the life of the party, but he proved to be sweet and remarkably easy to be with.

During the concert, she was glad of the opportunity to sit quietly and let the joyful strains of Mozart cascade over her, calming the turbulence of her thoughts. Memories of Stephen kept flashing through her mind—his eyes, his lips, his fingers. The music helped to shut him out.

Afterward, David took her out for a drink. He must have noticed at some point that she was staring rather dejectedly into her white wine, for he quietly asked, "Are you upset about something, Viola?"

Feeling guilty that she had let him see her abstraction, she replied, "I had a quarrel with someone earlier today. A friend of mine. It's been upsetting me a bit, yes. I'm sorry, David. I'm not very good company, I'm afraid."

He had kind brown eyes; they looked at her directly. "Would it make you feel better to talk about it?" he asked.

She shook her head. "No, I don't think so."

"A male friend?" he asked, his voice determinedly casual.

She met his eyes. "Yes. But it's not important. Would you order me another glass of wine?"

After that, she tried harder to be cheerful. They chatted about some of the people in the English department. Later, David remarked that he had enjoyed talking to Stephen Silkwood the night before.

"I asked him, you know, if he had really been disturbed by your review, since he made such an issue of it during the discussion. He hadn't, he admitted. Writers have to be impervious to negative criticism if they're going to survive, he said. He was just giving you a hard time."

"Oh, he was, was he? He's good at that." Bastard, she thought viciously.

"I thought it might make you feel better."

"Thanks, David, it does. Obviously Mr. Silkwood is as impervious as they come."

"I told him you were working on a biography of Percy Quentin. He knew Quentin well. Did you realize that, Viola? Even though you don't like the man, Silkwood might be an additional source for your biography."

"I don't need any additional sources for my biography. Percy Quentin was my father."

David stared at her in astonishment. "I didn't know that."

"It's not generally known," she said. Indeed, she had never told anyone at Whittacre that she was Quentin's daughter.

"My word, Viola, I'm a great fan of his, you know. I've read all his books. I liked almost all of them, particularly his last one, *An Intricate Solution*. Some critics thought he had softened his cynical attitudes too much, but I thought he'd humanized his characters in that story more than in any other. How sad to think he died at the height of his power."

Viola's face had gone crimson, and her heartbeat was

throbbing in her throat. "A lot of people didn't like *An Intricate Solution*," she said.

"Everybody I know liked it. I predict it will be remembered as one of his best. Is it true he struggled to write it as he lay crippled and dying?"

Viola was playing nervously with the stem of her wineglass. "He couldn't type, of course," she said. "I did all that for him."

"An amanuensis? Like Milton's daughters after he went blind?"

"Something like that."

Nothing made Viola more uneasy than talking about her father's final book. The truth was that she had done more than just type *An Intricate Solution*, the story of a suicidal young woman who arranges for her own death in such a way that her unfaithful lover is implicated as her murderer. Percy Quentin had been very ill at the time it was written, partly paralyzed from his stroke, and not always mentally competent. More than once his efforts to finish the novel had faltered. It never would have been published had it not been for Viola. It had been she who had urged him to do one final book at a time when he had seemed too depressed to write a word; she had gone through his old stories until she found a piece worthy of expansion. Once Percy got going on the project, he became enthusiastic, but, in the end, ill health claimed him before the manuscript was ready to go to press. Viola had rewritten the last couple of chapters and polished up the final draft.

After sending the manuscript off to Percy's publisher, she had had an attack of guilt about her active role in the writing of *An Intricate Solution*, wondering if she shouldn't simply have left it to a professional editor. No one knew about her contribution, and she wasn't eager to have anybody find out. Her sensitivity about this issue was the primary reason she had never told anyone at Whittacre that she was Percy's daughter.

David noticed Viola's uneasiness but attributed it to

the wrong cause. "He died just last summer, didn't he?" he asked gently. "You must miss him."

His words touched a chord of sorrow in her, and she took a long swallow of wine, thinking once again how deeply Stephen's remarks about her father had hurt her. Good riddance to him, she fumed inwardly. She didn't want to have anything to do with anyone who could speak as he had spoken about her father.

It was after midnight when David drove Viola home. She worried briefly about whether or not to invite him in; she didn't want any further sexual hassles tonight. Besides, although he was very nice, she simply wasn't attracted to David.

When he stopped his car in her driveway, she said, "Thank you, David. I was upset this evening, but you've made me feel almost lighthearted."

"Do you think, that is, would you like to spend another evening with me sometime?" he asked hesitantly.

"I—I don't know. I'm rather confused at the moment," she admitted. She felt that he was entitled to the truth, but she didn't want to hurt his feelings. "It's been awhile since I've dated, and I don't know exactly what I want."

Her voice must have sounded a little desperate, for David reached out boldly and squeezed her hands. "If you need a friend, you can call me any time," he offered. "I mean it. No strings attached. If you need to talk, I'm a good listener."

Her heart opened to him for his kindness. She leaned over and gently kissed his cheek. "Thank you, David," she whispered. "I'll remember that." Then she jumped out of the car and hurried into her house.

Tired and emotionally strung out, Viola rapidly undressed and got into bed. She had been asleep for about five minutes when the phone rang. Sitting up in bed, with her arm draped around her bare knees, she picked up the receiver from her bedside table. "Hello?"

"It's almost one o'clock in the morning," said a familiar voice. "Where the hell have you been?"

It was Stephen. He sounded just as angry and obnoxious as he'd been when he'd stormed out at seven. "I've been calling you all evening," he added.

"I was out," she rejoined, matching his tone. "At a concert."

There was a short silence. "With another man?"

"Yes, as a matter of fact. Do you have some objection?"

"Is he there with you now?"

She was hotly tempted to lie, but no words came.

"Put him on," Stephen said nastily, "and I'll give him a hint or two as to how to light your fire."

Viola furiously slammed down the phone. A few seconds later it rang again. She put the pillow over her ears and tried to ignore it, but on the sixteenth ring she couldn't stand it any longer. She snatched it up, but before she could speak, Stephen said in an entirely different tone, "I'm sorry. Don't hang up. I'm sorry, Viola."

"There's no one here with me," she said tautly, "but if there were, it would be no concern of yours. Just who do you think you are? I don't ever want to hear your voice again. I'm going to hang up and take the receiver off the hook, and tomorrow I'm going to get an unlisted number."

"I know where you live. You can't get rid of me that easily."

"You're the one who stalked out!"

"I know. I was an idiot, darling. I'm sorry. I regretted it before I was halfway home, and I've been calling you every fifteen minutes all evening to apologize."

He sounded sincere, but she was so surprised at this turn of events that she didn't know how to respond. Maybe his anger had cooled, but hers was still flaring!

"It should have been obvious to me just from the look on your face that you had no idea what I was talking about," he went on. He paused again, then said, "It didn't occur to me that you'd get yourself another date."

"Was I supposed to sit around all evening and cry over you?"

He sounded chagrined but calm. "I was worried about you, Viola. If you hadn't answered just now I was going to get back in the car and come check on you."

Her sarcasm continued unchecked. "Did you imagine I'd swallowed an overdose of sleeping pills on your account?"

"No, of course not. I was concerned, that's all, and I was going to drive over there. I can still drive over. If I leave now, I'll be there in an hour or so."

Her heart pattered like raindrops as she envisioned him beside her in bed, his long eyelashes darkly shadowing his sea-green eyes, his hands possessively exploring her body.

"In an hour or so I'll be sound asleep," she said shakily. "No, Stephen. I'm not taking any more rides on your emotional roller coaster tonight."

"Tomorrow?" he said hopefully.

"No. Look, it's obvious—isn't it?—that you and I don't get along. You hate my father, and you think I'm a bitch."

"I was overreacting," he admitted. "It's just that all these years, I believed . . . Oh, it was stupid of me; I realize that now. You were just a kid, too young to be a part of Percy's schemes. You really didn't receive any letters from me?"

"No, Stephen, and I logically concluded that you were simply using me. Taking advantage of a silly little girl who didn't yet know how to distinguish sincerity from empty promises."

"Viola, we need to talk."

"Every time we talk, we fight."

"Then maybe we should just shut up and make love," he said with a caress in his voice.

Her desire for him flared again in all its power. She couldn't answer; her throat ached from wanting him.

"I'm coming up there," he said impulsively. "Wait up for me."

"No, Stephen, please—" she protested, but to no avail.
The line went dead, leaving her staring at the receiver
in her hand as if it were about to bite her.

She threw back the covers and climbed out of bed to
pace around the room. What an impossible man: puz-
zlingly moody and thoroughly unpredictable. No one had
ever been able to do this to her. No one had ever reduced
her to such an agitated mass of emotion.

She went into the bathroom and stared at herself in
the mirror. Her loose hair was tangled from lying in bed,
and her blue eyes looked huge and passion-tinged. There's
passion there, all right, she told herself ruefully. Whether
the passion was anger or lust or even fear, she wasn't
entirely sure. All of them, probably. Damn him.

All of a sudden the corners of her mouth twitched,
and she broke out in a laugh. It was all so incredibly
ridiculous! It was one o'clock in the morning, and her
third date of the evening was coming to make love to
her. Unless they had another battle first.

Should she get dressed again? She was wearing only
a cotton nightshirt with the Whittacre College emblem
printed directly over her breasts—hardly the last word
in sensuality. He was coming to sleep with her. It would
be ludicrous to greet him fully dressed at two o'clock in
the morning, or whatever time it would be when he finally
arrived.

But she hadn't agreed to sleep with him. He had a
nerve to think she would. You're not going to sleep with
that man, Viola, she directed the sleepy-eyed redhead in
the mirror. Fiery hair does *not* always guarantee a fiery
nature.

Frowning, she turned away from the mirror, feeling
a disconcerting lack of rapport with her own image. She
wasn't at all certain what that fiery-haired creature would
do when Stephen Silkwood showed up again at her door.
She was turning out to be as unpredictable as he. There
was a locked self inside her somewhere, a trapped woman
of passion and warmth and laughter who had hidden her
face from the world after the wreck of her marriage and

the death of her father. Stephen had known that woman
once, and even claimed, spuriously, to have loved her.
Would she emerge again, for his sake? Would he treat
her just as callously this time if she did?

Back in her bedroom, Viola donned an imitation
Chinese silk robe with birds of paradise delicately printed
on it. She brushed her hair and dabbed a tiny bit of
perfume behind her ears and on her breasts, wrists, ankles, and thighs. She straightened the sheets on her bed
and looked at the clock. Only ten minutes had passed.
She didn't know exactly where he lived, or exactly how
long a drive he would have.

The phone rang.

"Viola? My car won't start," said Stephen, adding an
obscenity.

Her eyes shut in frustration.

"It must be the damp air. I had trouble with it last
night, too," he went on. "My house is miles from a gas
station, and it's the middle of the night. Darling, I'm
sorry. I never should have left."

"It's all right," she said mechanically. "It's better this
way. I'm really very tired. I wanted to call you back and
tell you not to come, but I didn't know where you lived."

"In Truro. On the Cape."

"You were going to drive all the way up from Truro
at this time of night?"

"It's not that far, and there wouldn't have been any
traffic." He thought a moment then added, "Listen, why
don't you come down? You have a car, I assume? I don't
know when I'll be able to get mine fixed, tomorrow being
Saturday. It's nice down here, Viola—sand, ocean, seafood. You'll love it. Get a pencil and I'll give you directions."

"No, Stephen," she said, willing herself to resist.

"My dear, there'll be hot cocoa waiting for you and
a fire on the hearth and an ardent lover in a warm bed."

Oh, no, she thought. The image was so tempting.

"Come for the weekend," he urged. "It's going to be
lovely and warm, they say. We can hike across the sand

dunes and bake clams and wade and sail and make love on the beach—" He stopped abruptly, then said it: "Just like the last time."

The last time. "Stephen, a few hours ago you looked and sounded as if you hated me. I don't understand this sudden turnabout. And besides"—she hesitated, then added—"you hurt me badly eleven years ago. I can't go through all that pain again."

"Do you think you were the only one to get hurt eleven years ago?" he asked, his voice harsh with emotion. "Would I have been so angry earlier this evening if I hadn't been just as deeply hurt as you?"

The idea had occurred to her, but she hadn't dared to give it credence. "You were so much older," she hedged. "More sophisticated, more experienced—"

"But not necessarily harder or less sensitive, Viola."

"We have to talk," she said, echoing his words of earlier.

"I know. Get into your car, darling, and come down."

"I'm too tired tonight, really. I'd drive off the road."

"Tomorrow, then. Get up early and come."

"I'll think about it."

"No, I want a commitment. A promise, a solemn vow." His voice roughened. "Or else I'll damn well hitchhike up there tonight."

Viola stared at the fingernails of her free hand, hesitating. "It's just for sex, isn't it," she finally said. "You want to sleep with me. You don't like me particularly. How could you? You hardly know me. I don't know why I'm even considering it, Stephen. I'm no good at casual affairs."

"What do you want, Professor, a love sonnet?" She recognized the tone of his lighthearted banter. "Most affairs start out casual. Get your sweet body down to the Cape, and we'll iron out the details later." He paused, then added more seriously, "Anyway, I do know you, Viola. However much we may have changed, we're both basically still the same people we were that summer at your father's cottage. We liked each other then. Why shouldn't we like each other now?"

But I'm not the same person, she thought miserably. That old self is a stranger to me now. When she spoke, it was to address a different issue. "I loved my father, Stephen," she said. "I don't believe what you said about his stealing a story from you."

His voice tightened. "I'll explain that."

"Please do."

"But not over the phone. It's a long story. If you want to hear it, you'll have to come here."

"That's blackmail."

He laughed softly. "No, Professor," he said devilishly, "that's seduction. The fact is, Viola, my love, your father could be Attila the Hun for all I care. Despite an occasional lapse, I'm not as obsessed by the past as you seem to think; it's the present I care about. Are you coming or not?"

When his voice was merry like that she couldn't resist him. "All right," she capitulated. "Give me the directions."

"Darling," he said, and she knew he was grinning.

The directions were complicated. As she finished writing them down, he added, "I'll have breakfast ready for you in the morning."

"Make it lunch. I intend to sleep late."

"Lunch then," he agreed meekly. "Good night, Viola. Dream of me."

"Arrogant male!" she teased him. "With any luck I'll go right to sleep and not dream at all."

But luck was not with her. She tossed feverishly in bed, repeatedly reliving each word, each caress. It was four o'clock in the morning before she was finally able to sleep, and her dreams were vividly erotic.

# CHAPTER
# *Five*

IT WAS A SUNNY, glorious day as Viola drove over the bridge to Cape Cod the next afternoon. At the end of the Cape Cod Canal she could see the hazy blue of the ocean sighing gently under a group of high, puffy clouds. It was warm for April, and she had her window rolled down. She was dressed casually, in blue jeans and a green cotton jersey, with a navy scarf knotted rakishly at her throat. Her hair, swinging loose over her shoulders, blew haphazardly in the wind.

Because it had taken so long for her to fall asleep the night before, she hadn't risen from bed until almost noon. She was going to be late, even for lunch, but she found pleasure in the idea of keeping Stephen Silkwood waiting.

She had nearly decided not to go at all. Again and again she'd reminded herself that she was not in the habit of leaping into bed with moody, melodramatic writers.

That was all he wanted with her, she was convinced. He had a passion for her, and even though he hated her father and suspected that she herself was unscrupulous, he was determined to gratify his need.

*Lustful* and *undisciplined* were the words he had used to describe himself. He wanted her.

She told herself that it was only her curiosity that was inducing her to keep their rendezvous. She had to know what he meant by those outrageous accusations against her father. She owed it to Percy to clear the matter up and to convince Stephen that her father had been a thoroughly creative writer who had never lifted an idea from anybody.

But she knew in her heart that that wasn't the only reason she was driving her car along the Mid-Cape Highway, smelling the sea and daydreaming of firm, tender hands on her body. *Lustful* and *undisciplined*. She had never thought those words would apply to her, but in this instance they did. She wanted him, too.

Still, desire was all it was, she told herself firmly. It had been a long time since she had indulged her natural longing for a physical relationship. She wasn't a nun, after all, but a normal young woman of twenty-eight. Other women had affairs. Other women didn't need to make a serious commitment before taking a lover. It would do her good, for once, to give herself the pleasure of an exciting weekend with an attractive man. She didn't have to be in love. Or so she kept telling herself.

The drive to Truro seemed endless. It was nearly at the tip of the Cape. The road narrowed, and the sand dunes and scrubby bushes were almost encroaching on the highway before she finally reached the turnoff.

She had to navigate more than one dirt road before she finally came to an old wooden sign that bore the name Silkwood. She turned into a sandy driveway that was covered with broken clam shells for traction.

The driveway curved around and came upon the house with a suddenness that startled her. She pulled up beside a gray BMW that had to be his. Last night he had left so quickly that she hadn't even gotten a good look at his car.

The house was on a hill overlooking the sea. It was modern—built since he had begun making money on his books, she guessed. A gray clapboard saltbox, it had huge plate-glass windows and solar panels in the sharply angled roof. A low deck encircled the entire house like a moat. Beyond the building stretched sand dunes and the wide blue arc of the sea.

As she parked her rather plebeian Chevy compact beside his spiffy BMW, Stephen appeared on the deck. He smiled and waved. He was clad in cutoff blue jeans, a gray sweat shirt, and a pair of battered running shoes.

With the grace of a trained athlete he vaulted over the railing of the deck and landed easily below in the sand. When she climbed out of her car he was there at her side, holding open the door. She noticed a wealth of tiny details at once: the warmth in his green eyes, the dark sprinkles of hair on his forearms where his sleeves were rolled up, the strong, sculpted muscles in his powerful legs.

"Hi," he said, grinning. "You're late." He didn't touch her.

"I overslept."

"I was beginning to think you'd lost your nerve." His eyes bored into hers, and his brows went up in a pleasant leer. "Venturing alone into the villain's lair after being unpardonably insulted and assaulted last night . . . You're a brave woman, Professor."

His eyes were sparkling, and a smile hovered about his sensuous, well-shaped lips. She sensed instantly that his good humor had returned. The mood was so different from the rage he had briefly exhibited in her home last evening. It freed her to respond in the same light tone.

"If you'd explored my house a little further instead of rushing off in a huff, you'd have discovered that I have drawers full of medals for bravery. My specialty is facing down angry, arrogant males."

He laughed. "Well, don't worry, I'm not angry anymore. I rarely stay mad for long. The arrogance, however, I'm afraid you're stuck with." He glanced into the rear seat of her car. "Where's your suitcase? In the trunk?"

She flushed slightly. "I didn't bring one." She had packed a suitcase but left it at home at the last minute. It seemed too obvious to show up with nightgown and toothbrush and clothes for another day. That was a victory she wasn't prepared to give him—not yet, at least.

"You don't care to admit the real reason you came, huh?" he said, reading her effortlessly.

Her eyes dropped under his stare. "Look, Stephen, I don't know what you expect, but—"

His tone as he interrupted was quietly kind. "I don't expect anything, Viola. Let's try to relax and be easy with each other, okay? It's a lovely day, and I've got two or three ideas about how to spend it, not one of which, believe it or not, includes lustfully assaulting you. I'm not totally devoid of other interests."

He spoke the last phrase with an almost boyish grin. The sea breeze lifted his dark, curly hair at his brow, revealing the strands of gray at his temples. He was a strange combination of the youthful and the mature, she thought. He dressed like a college kid and flew into rages like a child, yet there was a subtle control about him, too—a confidence and a steadiness that could only come with maturity.

He was looking at her intently, seeming to see into her heart and mind. It was not the appraising look a man gives to a woman he wants to sleep with, although that element was there; it was something infinitely more penetrating. Uneasiness swept her, and she stared distractedly out to sea. What did he want with her? she wondered nervously. What was this uncanny ability of his to breach her strongest defenses? Had she been a fool to come?

"Come up and see the house," he invited, slipping a casual arm around her shoulders but attempting no further intimacy. She walked with him up the flagstone path to the steps that led to the wide-planked deck. "Let me show you the view first," he said, leading her around to the ocean side of the building. "For everybody who comes here it seems to be *de rigueur* to gawk at the bay."

"It's worth gawking at," she said when she saw the smooth sands rolling down an incline to merge with the choppy blue sea. Green wisps of sand grass swelled back and forth on the dunes, ruffled by the stiff spring breeze. The air was clear and tangy. "What a marvelous place to write! I love the ocean."

"Well, there's one thing we have in common. So do I."

He opened the sliding door to the living room, and they went inside. The room was a large, airy oblong, entirely walled by glass on the ocean side. It was thickly carpeted in beige, and the modern, low-slung furniture was covered in maroons, golds, and other autumn tones. A huge brick island separated the living area from a small, spotless kitchen hung with copper pots and other gourmet cooking utensils, from which a delicious aroma was emanating.

"The beginning preparations for our supper," he said, in response to her questioning look. "You're a bit late for lunch, darling; I went ahead and ate without you. I hope you like seafood."

"I love it." She smiled archly as he was about to speak. "Something else we have in common?"

"So it seems. Seriously, if you're hungry, I can scare up some lunch for you."

"No, thanks, I ate before I left home. You like to cook?"

"I like to eat well, so I learned to cook. But I'm not fanatical about it." He cocked his head to one side. "I'm just trying to impress you, that's all."

"You're succeeding. I'm a rotten cook myself." She looked again at the impeccable surroundings and added, "You're a better housekeeper than I am, too. I should have left my shoes outside. I must be tracking sand all over your spotless carpet."

He laughed. "It's a good thing you were late or you'd

have caught me furiously vacuuming in your honor. Usually the place has more of that lived-in look. Come on, I'll show you the rest."

On that floor, besides the living room, dining room, and kitchen, which were demarcated by islands instead of walls, he showed her a bath and a small den. Upstairs there were three bedrooms and another bath. He showed her into the front bedroom, over the living room. It had the same glass walls and magnificent view, and it was dominated by a large, low water bed covered with a furry bedspread.

"This is my room," he said, his voice neutral but his eyes inviting.

"A water bed? I thought they went out years ago."

"Ever slept in one?"

"No, as a matter of fact."

"You'll like it. It has its limitations, of course—no bedposts. When we're in the mood for more piquant pleasures, we'll have to go to your place."

She flushed at the smug assumption of his tone, although she could not repress her thrill at the hint that making love with him would be exciting, to put it mildly.

"You seem to enjoy your sexual fantasies," she said dryly.

"My dear, I am an imaginative person. You must be, too, or you wouldn't earn your living dealing with literature. Why don't you sit down and tell me one of your sexual fantasies? You might find that we have more in common than you realize."

She retreated into the hall. "I thought you said you had other interests."

He followed her. "I do. But looking at you in those snug jeans is driving me crazy. And you're not wearing a bra under that jersey, are you." He came up against her and possessively ran a hand over her breasts. His other arm encircled her waist and pulled her close.

"I want you, Viola Quentin," he whispered urgently. "I couldn't sleep last night, imagining you here, in my house, in my bed...the things we would say...the things we would do. Kiss me."

His mouth came down on hers, and for a moment she allowed herself to respond with all the warmth that was pulsing through her fevered body. Then she realized what he had called her: Viola *Quentin*. It reminded her that nothing had been cleared up about her father's relationship with Stephen, not to mention her own.

She twisted her head to the side, breaking the exquisite contact with his lips. She half expected him to thread his fingers in her hair and force her mouth back to his in the domineering manner he had adopted last night, but it didn't happen. Instead he nuzzled her ear with his tongue and said, somewhat breathlessly, "I know. You want to hear my explanation first."

Once again she was surprised at the ease with which he could sense her feelings. She nodded. "Yes, I do. You accused my father of plagiarism. I'm not even sure what you were accusing me of, but it must have been serious or you wouldn't have slammed out the way you did."

"I slammed out because I was too angry to think straight. I was angry and frustrated and rather unnerved to discover that twice in my life I had fallen for your wretched father's daughter."

She pulled away from him, saying, "If you continue to insult him, I'll be the one to slam out today."

There was a pause while Stephen considered her. His tension was evident in the set of his mouth and the gleam of his green eyes behind his glasses. At last he said, "Look, he's your father, and he's dead. I can understand how you must feel. Nobody likes to hear anything unpleasant about his or her family. Let's just leave it. Let's not spoil our day together rehashing the past. I mean, who cares anyway? It's over and done with."

"I want to know what you think he plagiarized," she said stubbornly.

"A short story of mine."

"That's ridiculous. Your styles are totally different. Besides, he never would have done such a thing."

He shrugged. "No doubt it's all my fanciful imagination," he said sarcastically.

Viola could feel the anger in him. It wasn't as intense as last night's, but it was clearly there, and she felt a surge of resentment at the idea that something that had gone wrong eleven years ago between her father and Stephen should reach out of the past to sabotage her chance for happiness now. Perhaps he was right; perhaps it was futile to talk about the past. They weren't going to change each other's opinion of Percy's character no matter how much rehashing they did.

Stephen had turned and started ahead of her down the stairs to the living room, and she sensed that she wouldn't learn anything more from him now, even if she pressed. She decided not to argue. She had no wish to be in continual conflict with him. She wanted to relax and laugh and enjoy their time together.

She followed him downstairs and into the living room, where he stood staring broodingly out to sea. She came up behind him and slid her arms around his waist, tipping her chin against his shoulder. He turned instantly to take her in his arms, and she could see the surprise and pleasure in his eyes as she raised her lips to his in a peace offering.

"Don't worry, sweetheart," he said when the lingering kiss ended. "We'll work this thing out somehow or other. In the meantime, how about a jog along the beach?"

"Okay," she agreed, pulling free and dashing for the sliding door that led outside. Over her shoulder she gave him a challenging grin. "I'll race you to the water."

"You'll lose." He laughed and followed her.

The afternoon passed quickly and pleasantly. After jogging, Viola and Stephen hiked a couple of miles along the deserted beach, passing numerous boarded-up summer homes. Few people besides Stephen lived here all year long. "I need solitude when I write," he explained. "I never get much done in the summer when the neighbors show up."

When they got back to his beachfront, they sat down under the hot sun to construct an elaborate sand castle. He wanted its architecture to be modern, but she insisted on medieval style. When she attempted to construct flying buttresses out of wet sand, Stephen rolled onto his stomach and laughed at her until he choked. The buttresses did not fly for long. The tide began to rise and threatened to breach the castle walls.

"I can't bear to stay and watch it destroyed," she lamented.

"We'll go in, then. I've got to check the food anyway."

Her hair was tangled from the wind, and there was sand and salt all over her, so she chose to stay out on a chaise longue on the deck while Stephen attended to the cooking. The sun was sinking, and the afternoon was taking on a distinct chill, but it felt so good to be breathing the sea air that she wanted to relish it as long as she could. Staring at the waves as they rolled in, one after another, she allowed the sound and smell of the ocean to suck her into the past.

She knew now why she had been so devastated by Stephen's disappearance from her life eleven years before. It had not been merely a teenage romance. She had deeply and sincerely loved him. And the things she had loved about him then she still loved about him now: his quick wit, his liveliness, the uninhibited way he expressed his emotions. Besides, despite the sexual tension and the uncertainty about his relationship with her father, she felt inexplicably easy with him. She couldn't describe it exactly; it was as though there were an instinctive stream of communication flowing between them, making them unusually sensitive to each other's thoughts and feelings.

On the surface, the communication wasn't always perfect; it certainly hadn't been last night. But this afternoon they had talked smoothly and empathetically with no difficulty at all.

He brought her a drink and settled his long limbs into a chaise beside her. She had asked for a martini, and he had made it very dry. It looked like a double. She raised her eyebrows and asked him if he was trying to get her drunk.

"Of course." He grinned, his eyes sweeping over her. "Hungry?"

"Starved."

"So am I. I'm wondering, however, which appetite to satisfy first." His hand reached over and slid along the downy flesh of her arm, then he squeezed her wrist lightly with his fingers. Her entire body leaped into arousal at his touch. "Dinner will be another twenty minutes. Is that long enough, do you suppose?"

She couldn't pretend that she didn't understand. "Not for a woman," she said airily.

"Ah, so you expect satisfaction, do you?" He looked amused. "Perfection the first time?"

"No, not necessarily. Why? Are you nervous?"

"Yes, aren't you?"

She was, of course, but she'd hardly expected him to be. "You're joking."

"You think I'm too suave and sophisticated to be nervous?"

She eyed his cutoffs and his threadbare sweat shirt, mentally comparing him with his hero, Maxwell Trencher, who dressed in expensive designer suits and carried his lethal weapons around in an Italian leather briefcase. "Suave and sophisticated you're not," she said, laughing.

He made a show of looking insulted. "What do you mean, suave and sophisticated I'm not? I'll have you know I've jetted with the jet set and cozied up in chic hideaways with some of the most beautiful of the Beautiful People. My former wife was wealthy and well connected. Even after she divorced me, I continued to run with those crowds for a while."

"Why did she divorce you?" Viola asked.

He shrugged, sipping his drink, but she noticed that his face had tightened and his eyes had turned cold. He let go of her hand. "She fell for another man," he said shortly.

"I see," Viola said sympathetically. "Did she marry him?"

He gave her a surprisingly hostile glare. "No. She was just acting out her Oedipal feelings with the guy. He was many years her senior. It didn't last. She married someone else."

Viola felt a twinge of jealousy. She assumed, from the bitterness of his tone, that he still had feelings for his ex-wife. "How come you never remarried?" she persisted. "Did she destroy your faith in women forever?"

His mood seemed to lighten a little. "You imagine I hate all women because my wife dumped me eleven years ago?"

"I don't know. Have you ever analyzed your exact relationship with your misogynistic creation, Maxwell Trencher?"

"You're not going to start that again, are you? Haven't I convinced you that Max and I are different? I haven't committed a single act of brutality all afternoon."

She smiled, but her uneasiness remained. She couldn't help thinking back to some of the passages she had found particularly objectionable in Stephen's novels. The women Max brutalized were always "bad guys"—either murderers themselves or associates of murderers—but the supposed morality of his acts seemed rather spurious to her. No doubt the general reader came away with the feeling that Max's victims had gotten what they deserved, but the fact remained that Max derived a vast amount of sadistic pleasure from taking justice into his own hands. She wondered if Stephen identified with Max as he wrote the scenes.

"I'm interested in the way authors relate to their characters," she went on. "Max beats up women in an age when beating up women is frowned upon. Yet your books sell phenomenally well. Why? Do all men secretly desire to beat up women?"

"You're obsessed with the subject, aren't you? Why? Do you imagine I'm going to turn into the Marquis de Sade tonight and come after you with a whip?"

Viola shifted uncomfortably. She wished he wouldn't even joke about violence toward her. It reminded her too vividly of Douglas.

"Viola?" he said in a different tone when she didn't respond. "What is it? You don't really believe I'd do anything to hurt you, do you?"

She was gazing out to sea, avoiding his eyes. "I left my husband because he physically attacked me. I initiated divorce proceedings from a shelter for battered wives."

Her voice was calm, almost impersonal, but Stephen's rang with emotion as he found a harsh, explicit term to describe her ex-husband. A moment later he used a similar term to describe himself. "I should have guessed," he said. "No wonder you hate Max."

There was an awkward pause. Why had she told him? Viola asked herself. She had never told anybody before.

With a shiver she remembered the horror of that night, and without consciously willing it, she heard her voice continuing to recount the disaster to Stephen, as if it were something she finally had to get off her chest.

"He was my teacher...I met him the year I started graduate school. We were married the next summer, but it soon became obvious that our love of literature was all we had in common. I had to change my entire lifestyle for him, because he didn't enjoy getting together with friends, or dining or dancing or movies, even. He was quiet, serious, not the least bit gregarious."

"Why on earth did you marry him?" Stephen interrupted.

"I've asked myself that same question over and over. I suppose the fact that he was my mentor had a lot to do with it. He had a certain power over me. I was stupid then, and young—only twenty-two. He was forty. I suppose I was flattered that he wanted me. Anyway, it was a mistake, and I paid for it—dearly."

Stephen's fingers had laced with hers again, and she found their firmness comforting. "You don't have to talk about it if you don't want to," he said.

"I don't know why, but I want to tell you. Anyway, it's not what you think. He wasn't brutal to me all the time. In fact, it wasn't until the final night we were together that he ever struck me. He was insecure, you see, and very jealous. He suspected me of being unfaithful to him with men my own age, and he accused me of it on the slightest provocation. I wasn't unfaithful, ever, and his insinuations infuriated me. I tried to get him to consent to marital counseling, but he absolutely refused.

"Finally, on that last awful night, I returned home early from a canceled class and discovered him in bed with another one of his students. You can imagine how I felt. All his accusations, and he was the one betraying the marriage. I couldn't believe it.

"He got rid of the girl, and we screamed at each other—or at least I screamed at him. I have a temper just like yours, Stephen, but Douglas was always so cool and collected. Until that night I hadn't been the least bit afraid of him physically, which was why it was so frightening when he suddenly lost control of himself and started hitting me."

She closed her eyes, reliving the scene in her mind and feeling once again her terror, shock, and pain. Stephen's grip on her hand tightened, and he murmured something gentle and reassuring.

"He went berserk," she added. "I thought he was going to kill me."

There was another silence, during which Viola felt Stephen's sympathy washing over her in waves, without words, without more than the pressure of his hand on hers.

"How did you get away?" Stephen asked quietly.

"I managed to hit him on the head with a candlestick

and run out of the house. It was the middle of the night by then, and I wandered aimlessly for a while until I remembered the shelter I'd read about in the newspaper a few days before. The women at that shelter were great. They took me in and calmed me down—I was totally hysterical—and by morning I knew I wanted a divorce. They put me in touch with a lawyer, and I never looked back."

"Until tonight?"

She was nodding in response when his expression darkened and he added, "Or was it last night that made you look back?"

"Last night?"

"When I lost my temper and turned briefly into Max before your startled eyes." He paused. "Will you tell me something, Viola? Honestly?"

She raised her eyebrows quizzically at the seriousness in his voice. "I'll try. What?"

"If you're afraid of men—as nobody could blame you for being after what Douglas did to you—then what the hell are you doing here with me?"

# CHAPTER
## *Six*

SITTING ON STEPHEN'S deck with the sound of the sea in her ears and his words ringing in her brain, Viola sought for an answer to his question.

"I don't understand," she said at last. "Are you implying that the circumstances of my divorce make it impossible for me to trust another man?"

"I don't know." His fingers were still firmly holding hers. "But before we venture any deeper into this relationship, I'd like to find out."

"Don't worry, Stephen, I won't go to pieces on you. I promise," she said sarcastically. She felt annoyed for some reason, and his use of the word *relationship* didn't help matters. Did he really want a relationship with her? Or was it only sex he was interested in? She abruptly withdrew her hand.

"Don't pick another fight with me," he warned. "I'm not the least bit worried that you'll go to pieces. You're obviously one tough and gutsy lady. I'm feeling guilty about the way I've treated you so far, that's all. My behavior has been aggressive from the start, and my self-indulgent display of anger at your place last night must have frightened you."

"You can put away the kid gloves," she assured him. "Honest anger openly displayed doesn't frighten me. Douglas didn't show his feelings. When he blew up that night it was like watching Jekyll turn into Hyde. You're not like that; at least, I don't think you are."

"I'm not Douglas—or Max, for that matter," he agreed. "Max is a fiction; he sells books. I've never shot, raped, or beaten a woman in my life."

"I didn't seriously think you had." She reflected a moment, then added, "But it's true your behavior has been aggressive, and I'm not sure how I feel about that."

"What do you mean you're not sure? Obviously you hate it."

She frowned. "Then why am I here?"

Stephen's face was transformed by a mock-villainous grin. "Because deep down you like aggressive men?" he suggested. "You're not exactly a shrinking violet yourself, darling. As long as I don't pose a physical threat to you, you're quite happy to take me on."

"You may be right," she admitted, slanting a mischievous look at him from under her thick eyelashes. "Why do I get the feeling that you're about to pose a physical threat?"

*"Invitation,* not *threat* is what I'm about to pose," he returned. "If I act masterful, it's simply to excite us both." He paused, his gaze roving over her body. "I won't deny that I enjoy that role. But if it frightens you," he hastened to add, "I won't do it."

"It doesn't frighten me, as long as it's only a fantasy," she said, struggling to match his honesty with her own. "What happened with Douglas was no fantasy. It was a brutal attempt to dominate me in the only way that was left to him. It was hostile and hurtful—an act of violence."

"I could never treat you like that, Viola," he said gently.

"Good, because whatever doubts I had about the matter at the age of twenty-two, or seventeen, for that matter, I know now that I can't bear to be dominated by any man."

His deep green gaze caressed her. "Fair enough. I promise not to dominate you—except in bed."

The sexual current leaped between them. Viola moistened her lips with her tongue. "Suppose I want to dominate *you* in bed?"

"We take turns?" he offered, laughing. "It's my turn first, love. After we've finished dinner I intend to drag you upstairs to my water bed, strip off all your clothes, and force you to gratify every bizarre desire that comes into my head." He treated her to a leer that made her tingle all the way to her fingertips. "Is that agreeable to you?"

"Yes," she whispered with a provocative smile. He uncoiled himself from his chair and leaned over to kiss her, his lips hard and firm against her own. As the kiss deepened, he pulled her up into his arms and ran his hands along her spine to the curve of her bottom.

"Umm, nice," he murmured, molding her thighs to fit his own. "Can you feel me wanting you?"

She nodded, shivering with excitement at her consciousness of his arousal. Her body began to glow with desire.

"I don't know how I've waited all day," he added huskily, kissing her throat, then moving his lips to nibble delicately at the portal of her ear. Her hands in turn explored his tautly muscled shoulders, then slid down to his waist and slipped under the sweat shirt to caress the bare skin of his back. He groaned and crushed her harder against him, his lips claiming hers once again, his tongue deeply invading the warm cavern of her mouth.

"Stephen," she whispered against his lips, taking pleasure in the sweet syllables of his name.

One of his hands reached out and opened the glass

doors, and he urged her into the living room and toward the nearest couch. But before they reached it the oven timer went off.

"Damn. Dinner's ready. What do we do—ruin the food or torture ourselves with more waiting?"

She couldn't have cared less about dinner at that point, except for the fact that he had gone to the trouble of cooking it. "Will it really be ruined?"

"By the time I'm done with you, yes." He pulled back a little, still holding her loosely around the waist. "We're going to take our time about this, Viola. I want to savor every moment." He nodded at the table set for two in the candlelit dining room. "Besides, I've already poured the wine." His smile widened to a grin as he ran a finger over her desire-haunted face. "Control yourself, wench. You'll have me soon enough."

Laughing, she pushed him away and went to sit at a place set with sterling silver and delicate, gold-rimmed china. Taking a sip of her wine, she reminded herself to go easy on it. She didn't want to be out of her senses with alcohol when he took her upstairs. She, too, wanted to savor every moment.

Dinner was delicious. After a spicy bouillabaisse, he served her stuffed clams and tender white rice steamed with currants and pignolia nuts, accompanied by a spinach salad and glazed baby carrots. They had raspberry mousse for dessert. When she finally pushed away the last plate and sipped her coffee, she felt a pleasant satiety of one appetite, at least.

"You can cook for me any time."

"You really liked it?"

"I loved it."

"Well, that's something," he said, observing the empty serving dishes with satisfaction. "Because impressing you is a helluva lot of work. I slaved over a hot stove all morning!"

"You relax. I'll do the dishes."

She got up and carried a stack of plates to the kitchen area. As she placed them in the sink, Stephen came up behind her and put his arms around her, his hands running over her hips and stomach before sliding up under her jersey toward her breasts.

"Later," he said thickly. "I've waited long enough." The tip of his tongue touched the back of her neck, and she thrilled with little goose bumps of pleasure. Revolving in his arms until they were face to face, she lifted her moistened lips for his kiss. But instead of accepting her unspoken invitation, he swept her into his arms and carried her toward the stairs.

"Very romantic," she purred as he mounted the steps to his bedroom. "But I'm too heavy. You'll hurt your back, and then where will we be?"

"No problem," he murmured, brushing her lips with his. "Water beds are great for hurt backs. I'll just have to stay there, for the foreseeable future, while you nurse me back to health."

He set her down in the middle of his bedroom opposite the huge windows with the magnificent view of the sea. A full moon was rising over Cape Cod Bay, silvering the black water and slanting its light into the dark corners of his room.

"It's beautiful," she whispered.

"Don't stare at it. It'll make you crazy."

"A lunatic?" she smiled. "As in the old folk legends?"

He was stripping off his sweat shirt. The sight of his naked, hair-covered chest sent new waves of desire coursing through her.

"Yes, look at me, bathed in moonlight every night and wrapped in a fantasy world most of my waking hours. All writers are a little crazy, darling. Don't you know that?"

"I know it," she said wryly. "After growing up with one."

As soon as the words were out, she regretted them. This was not the moment to conjure up the memory of Percy Quentin. But Stephen took it lightly, advancing with a smile and placing his hands on her shoulders.

"Are you by any chance reminding me that you're an

antagonistic reviewer and Percy Quentin's daughter? Are you sure that's wise, darling?"

"It doesn't seem to disturb you," she whispered.

His eyes glittered. "No, I like a challenge, crimson-top. Nothing like a foray into the enemy camp to get the blood moving faster in the veins."

"I'm not behaving very much like an enemy," she said with a laugh. She reached out and tugged at the wiry black hair on his chest until he winced. "There. Feel my artillery?"

His hands slid underneath her jersey, seeking her breasts. In an instant he was cupping them, molding them, his thumbs flicking back and forth over her nipples, which hardened to sensitive peaks. "You won't be so smug when you feel my sword," he retorted.

She giggled, but her laughter was choked off by a surge of helpless eroticism as he lifted her jersey and pulled it over her head, exposing her breasts to the moonlight and his eyes. After a long, passionate gaze that made her tingle with anticipation, he bent his head and began sucking one of her nipples until she writhed in his arms, her legs so weak with longing that she could hardly stand.

"Stephen," she murmured, encouraging him to increase the pace of his lovemaking. Her nails lightly traced a path down the flesh of his stomach to the belt of his jeans.

"Do you want me, darling?" His breath was warm against her tingling breast. His teeth closed on the nipple, bearing down gently until she felt a tender hub of delicious excitement. She moaned and arched against him, feeling with a thrill the ridge of his fully aroused manhood through the barrier of denim.

"Yes," she gasped, her voice urgent with longing. "Yes, Stephen, yes. I want you."

He released her and stepped back a foot or so. "Then strip off the rest of your clothes, darling. Slowly," he ordered.

She was suddenly conscious of the enormous uncur-

tained window. Even though there was no one but him
to see her, she felt embarrassed. "I can't," she protested.

"Do it," he growled.

He was in one of his fantasy roles, she knew instinctively. She felt no fear, only excitement. Her entire body
was moist and hot, and there was an ache between her
legs. Drawing a deep breath, she unsnapped her jeans
and slid out of them as sensuously as she could. Stephen
whistled softly when he saw her long, slender legs, and
her soft hips, covered only by a brief pair of bikini panties.

"Keep going."

"It's your turn to take something off."

Raising his eyebrows, he coolly stripped away his
cutoff jeans, and she saw that he wasn't wearing under-
shorts. He stood before her, naked and ready to love her,
his lanky body as tense and hard as rock.

Trembling, she pulled down her panties and stepped
out of them. "Sexy lady," he whispered. His eyes moved
slowly over her nakedness, making her feel worshiped,
like a pagan goddess. "The moon is caressing your body,
making me jealous."

He stalked over to the bed, tugging her after him with
a firm grip on one wrist. With a quick jerk he pulled off
the fur bedspread. "Lie down," he commanded, pushing
her onto the low, strangely rolling luxury of the water-
filled mattress. It felt warm beneath her bare skin, and
it made a soft, flowing sound as it adjusted to her curves.

"I'm not protected," she told him as he tore off his
glasses and settled down beside her. She was a little
dazed at the risk she was taking. She couldn't remember
another time when she'd ever been so overcome with
passion as to be thoughtless of the consequences. Stephen
seemed to have turned her mind to jelly.

"Don't worry," he reassured her. "I'll take care of it."
And the drift of his exquisite hands over her naked flesh
soon quieted her anxiety.

He turned her over onto her stomach and explored her

back with the tips of his fingers, then with his lips. As his mouth moved gently along her backbone, delighting her with hundreds of feathery kisses, he murmured against her, "Does that mean there's no other lover in your life?"

She rolled over, somewhat annoyed. The bed heaved, disorienting her slightly. "Am I acting as if there's another lover?"

"What about the guy last night?"

For a moment she drew a blank. Stephen had so captivated her attention that she had forgotten all about David Newstead. "Oh, him," she said casually.

He ran his fingers over her breasts and down to her softly rounded belly. "Yes, him. Who is he?"

"Nobody special."

His hand moved lower, tantalizing her by circling but not touching the hollow between her legs. Of their own volition, her hips arched toward his hand, and he smiled. "Come now, a beautiful, sexy woman like you? With brains and wit to boot? The men must be lining up for tickets."

"I don't issue tickets," she retorted. "I value my independence too much to engage in a lot of distracting love affairs."

"A point worth making," said Stephen, his tone serious. "So do I." His fingers found her, probed her, and she cried out faintly in her longing. He bent his head and tongued one of her nipples. "And so, my casual weekend love, let us make the most of the time we have together."

His words whispered a warning in some dark corner of her brain, but she was too wound up with desire to heed it. The future would have to take care of itself. All she could deal with was the here and now, when she had to have his body joined to hers, fulfilling her, completing her.

Her impatient hands stroked him, glorying in his strength, his hardness. Her fingernails traced sensuous patterns on his back, dug into the flesh of his buttocks, and caressed him intimately until he groaned his pleasure.

Smiling seductively, she pulled him against her lower body and urged him to end the torment for both of them. He shuddered in her arms; she knew he could feel the welcoming warmth between her parted legs.

But he was not to be hurried. "Tell me what you like," he murmured huskily, pulling away slightly and finding the center point of her passions with his clever, delicate fingers. "I want to please you, sweetheart. Like this? Harder? Tell me, love."

So she told him, in a low voice strained with desire, and was astonished to discover that verbalizing the experience excited her further. Douglas had never inquired into her sexual feelings, expecting her to be gratified by whatever caresses he chose to favor her with. Stephen was a far more caring lover. He controlled his own response—and the raggedness of his breathing revealed it was no easy task—in order to build her to an intensity of sensation that left her quivering on the edge of fulfillment.

"You're so responsive," he muttered delightedly, covering her with his sweat-damp, eager body. "So warm, so sweet... Viola, darling, I've waited eleven years for you. Forgive me, but I don't think I can wait any longer. Are you ready for me, sweetheart?"

"Yes," she whispered hoarsely. "Now, Stephen, please!"

He rolled away from her for a moment, and when he returned there was a faint look of uneasiness about him. He leaned up over her, the water bed swaying with his shifting weight, and said, "There's something I probably ought to tell you first."

"What?" she demanded, alarmed at the hint of guilt in his eyes. For a second she expected some awful revelation: he was married again, or in love with another woman, or...

"It's about the story Percy stole from me," he said. "You see, there's this article I've been trying to write, and—"

"Oh, dear God, Stephen, not *now*," she protested. "Just come to me quickly before I go mad!"

He grinned and kissed her hungry mouth, then let himself down until she could feel the pressure of his maleness ready to penetrate her depths. "Okay, Professor," he said teasingly, smoothing her body with long, stroking caresses that turned her into an elemental being who seemed to have no connection to the ordinary world. She didn't recognize herself in the writhing, shuddering creature who cried out over and over for him to take her. Even so, he continued to delay, clearly tantalizing himself as well as her with his slowness, then losing control abruptly and moving into her in a frenzy of primitive possession.

They rocked together, the water bed echoing their frantic rhythms, rolling in hard waves beneath them, bouncing them more deeply into one another and heightening their already raging pleasure. Viola reached the summit just before he did and laughed aloud with the exhilarating joy of the moment. His pleasures were quieter but felt every bit as intense.

Afterward they lay still, limbs entwined and bathed in moonlight while the water bed still rippled beneath them. Viola was drained of every emotion except a delicious sense of ease.

His lips against her hair, Stephen finally spoke. "Do you always laugh when you're..."

"No," she replied. "It's just that I felt so absurdly happy, so completely alive."

"I've never known a woman who giggled at that particular moment," he said. "You're quite an original." His voice was affectionate. "Not to mention sexy as hell." His hands were still gently fondling her. "It was worth the wait," he added, kissing her.

"For me, too," she said. "You needn't have been nervous. It *was* perfection the first time."

"How could it be otherwise with such a sensuous moon goddess in my bed?" he said, sweeping loving hands over her moonlight-bathed flesh.

"You're pretty sexy yourself," she said, losing her fingers in his thick, curly hair.

"I know," he said modestly, his grin a silver-white flash in the moonlight. "I issue tickets."

# CHAPTER
## Seven

THE SKY WAS beginning to lighten faintly with the coming of the dawn when Viola awakened and stumbled to Stephen's bathroom. She felt dazed from lack of sleep and the satiety of love. It had been only a couple of hours since she and Stephen had finally settled down to doze, tightly wrapped in each other's arms. All through the night they had alternately made love and talked, conversing animatedly on an endless variety of subjects. Viola had learned the plot of Stephen's latest mystery novel; he'd heard all about her life at Whittacre. The only thing they had not discussed was the past.

Viola splashed cold water on her face and examined herself in the mirror over the sink. Her hair was a wild and flaming mess, and her eyes, though sleepy-looking, were glowing with satisfaction and peace. Her cheeks were flushed from the roughness of Stephen's overnight growth of beard.

Spontaneously, she smiled at herself in the mirror. She looked utterly happy. And why not? She was in love.

No one had ever made her feel the way Stephen did. Their bodies were perfect together, but it was more, much more than that. Something had magically slipped into place, as if a mysterious hand had put together all the random jigsaw pieces of her life and produced a complete and shining whole. They were made for each other; of that there could be no doubt. Although he had not explicitly said so, she was sure he felt it, too.

Still smiling, Viola went back into the bedroom and stood looking down at her lover sleeping on the water bed. He lay sprawled on his back, half covered by the fur bedspread, one arm stretched out as if unconsciously seeking her. The sculpted bones of his face seemed much less harsh than when he was sarcastic or angry. His entire expression was peaceful, like hers, and the lines of tension around his eyes and mouth had been wiped away. He looked young, far younger than his years.

She was about to crawl back into bed beside him when she noticed the rosy hue extending out over the ocean, the forerunner of the sunrise, which she hardly ever saw. She was a night person, staying up late and rarely awakening before seven-thirty in the morning. This morning the rising sun suddenly seemed to symbolize the new life that her love for Stephen was going to bring, and she wanted to watch it break out of the purple sea.

Because it was chilly, she retrieved her blue jeans from the heap of clothes on the floor beside the bed and pulled them on over her nakedness. Then, with a possessive grin, she picked up Stephen's sweat shirt and drew it over her head. It was much too big for her, but she took a subtle pleasure in wearing something that had touched his body last night.

She went to the circular staircase at the end of the bedroom. She had noticed it last night and asked Stephen what was up there, and he'd explained that the entire third story consisted of one large room, his study, which was dominated by large windows. She wanted to see where he composed his novels, where he did all his work. It was also likely to be the best place from which to watch the dawn.

The view was even more spectacular than she had imagined. The tide was high, and a strong wind ripped across the waves, creating thousands of foamy whitecaps beneath the pearly predawn sky. In the east, the sea was already a rolling carpet of hot pink and apricot, even though the sun had not yet made its appearance. Viola pulled Stephen's desk chair away from the typewriter table and sat down to watch. As the crimson sun slowly burst from the sea, she felt her spirits lift with it until her soul was a pure and shining flame within her. She wished Stephen could be with her to feel it, too, but she hadn't the heart to wake him.

She remained at the window in a kind of meditative trance until the sun was well over the horizon. Then, yawning, she rose to go back downstairs. But first she pushed the chair back over to Stephen's desk, lingering briefly to examine the place where he spent so much of his time. There was a large pile of typed pages on one side of the desk—his latest manuscript, she supposed—and a stack of blank paper and carbon arranged neatly beside his typewriter. On top of the typewriter was a thinner pile, ten or twelve pages, perhaps. The latest chapter? Stephen was stuck; he had told her so last night. Max had gotten himself into a messy situation, and Stephen didn't know how to get him out. She picked up the pages and started to flip through them.

It took her a couple of seconds to realize that she wasn't holding a chapter from a mystery novel, but the rough draft of a critical article, not unlike the sort of thing she wrote. A name leaped out at her: Percy Quentin.

Embarrassed, she laid the typescript down on the desk. Whatever it was, she didn't think she had the right to read it without Stephen's permission. Her heart had begun to beat uncomfortably hard in her chest. "There's this article I've been trying to write," he'd told her, looking guilty as hell, but she had refused to let him discuss Percy Quentin. She hadn't wanted any possible source of dissension to ruin their first night of love.

The temptation to see what he was writing was overwhelming, and she had to force her eyes to look away. Her glance fell instead on a letter that was also lying on the desk. It bore the letterhead of a well-known periodical, and before she could stop herself her brain had taken in the opening words of the letter: "Dear Mr. Silkwood: Concerning your query about doing a piece on the alleged plagiarism of one of your plots, we would be happy to take a look at your article, along with your documentation . . ."

Having read that far, she was lost. She sat down and scanned the rest of the letter, which went on to offer to buy his article for a thousand dollars if the editors thought he thoroughly proved his case. Her face was flushed, and her hands were shaking as she put down the letter and picked up the article again. There was no going back now; she had to read it to understand these ridiculous charges. As she read, the pounding of her heart intensified.

There was a sound behind her, and she jolted half out of the chair. Stephen was standing at the top of the staircase, gloriously naked, staring at her with undisguised fury in his eyes. "What the hell are you doing?" he demanded hoarsely. He looked and sounded the way he had the other night at her house when he'd discovered who she was and lost his temper.

But this time her temper, too, was raging. She had read only three paragraphs, but it was plain what he was doing—destroying her father's reputation!

She flung the article at him, editor's letter and all. "You bastard!" she cried. "So this is what you meant. I never dreamed it would be anything so low, Stephen, or so full of slander and lies!"

He advanced on her and picked up the manuscript from the floor where she had thrown it. "How dare you come up here and poke around in my things!" he shouted back.

"It's a good thing I did. My father never stole an idea in his life. No wonder you refused to talk about him all day yesterday, with this hot little item in your typewriter. When were you going to tell me? After it came out in print? After you got the money, which I'm sure you so desperately need?" Her voice was furiously sarcastic. "Or did you plan to tell me today, by the harsh light of morning, after I'd spent the whole night gratifying your passions in bed? Does it increase your pleasure to know that you've finally made a fool of Percy Quentin's daughter? Does it sweeten your revenge?"

She was so angry she hardly knew what she was saying, but he stood there, a couple of feet away from her, listening to every bitter word. His eyes were hard as glass, and as she flung the last question at him, the lines around his mouth tightened and his fingers clenched into fists.

"Yes," he answered brutally. "Nothing would have irritated Percy more than to know I finally seduced his precious daughter. He kept me away from you eleven years ago, but this time he wasn't around to protect you, was he."

"You bastard," she repeated. Her anger faded slightly, and she felt as if she might start to cry. "I trusted you," she said faintly. "You mean you made love to me only to get back at my father? My father, who's dead? What kind of twisted mentality could motivate such behavior, Stephen? Lord! You seemed so affectionate, so sweet last night . . . just like the last time." She put her head in her hands, rocking back and forth in misery. "How could I have been such a fool?"

There was a long silence; then he stepped closer, and she felt his hands begin to stroke her hair. "Viola—"

"Don't touch me!"

"I did try to tell you. Remember? Last night before we made love? You wouldn't listen."

"You should have tried a little harder!"

His voice was gentler now, and he had not taken away his hands, which were tenderly smoothing her hair back from her face. "Look, darling, I know this hurts. It must be a nasty shock to read such things about your father, and for that I'm sorry."

She wasn't convinced. "Oh, sure. You love it." She cast a glance at his carefully controlled expression, seeing plainly that he had deliberately leashed his anger. Irresistibly, her eyes moved down over his lean, angular body, the wiry hair springing from his muscled chest, the tension of his strong thighs, and the undisguised fact that he still desired her. "Look at you. You're glittering with sadistic satisfaction. I should have known it from the moment you mauled me in the elevator. You're totally warped, Stephen. You knew if you showed me this piece of trash yesterday I'd never have slept with you."

"Yes," he admitted, "I knew that. I can't deny it. But I've never wanted anyone so badly. No woman has ever torn at me the way you do, Viola. Please, forget about Percy and come back to bed."

"You must be crazy! I want an explanation of this pack of lies, Stephen. How could you have written this calumny, much less sold it to a journal?"

"It's not a pack of lies. If you've read the article you'll have to acknowledge that I prove my case."

"I've read enough to know that you're writing fiction, as always."

"Read it all, Viola. Go on." He thrust the article at her. "Take it, dammit, and read it."

With a glare she grabbed the sheaf of paper out of his hand and settled down to read. Stephen rummaged around in a drawer and threw in front of her an old typewritten manuscript and a copy of one of her father's novels, flipped open to reveal several underlined passages. The documentation, she supposed.

As she read, Viola's stomach began to feel queasy. When she got to the last page, she looked up at him, her face white. The novel he had given her was *An Intricate*

*Solution,* her father's last book, which she herself had edited and prepared for publication.

"One of my first mysteries was a short story about a suicidal woman who frames her unfaithful lover for her own death. I gave a copy of it to Percy to evaluate, and he blasted the writing to pieces. I was young; I respected his literary judgment. I put the story away, convinced it was no good.

"I loved your father, Viola," he went on intensely. "My own father died when I was fifteen, and I was always looking for paternal figures to replace him. Percy was happy enough to play the role I'd cast him in, for a while. When it ended—when I found out what he was really made of—I was hurt and bitter, but it didn't change my opinion of him as a writer.

"Then, two months ago, what did I see? Percy's post-humous novel appears, the entire plot structure of which he ripped off from my immature manuscript. Apparently my short story improved with age."

He paused for a moment, and Viola again buried her face in her hands. Now, *now* it made sense. Dear God, it made too much sense now.

"Study the passages I've indicated," he continued, "and study the manuscript of my story. The names have all been changed, and the story line filled out and developed, but the basic plot is the same and the 'intricate solution' is identical. The apparent murder proves to have been a suicide, and the lover gets off. It's my story, Viola, not Percy's."

She didn't take the material he held out to her. She didn't have to. She recognized his manuscript now, having seen a copy of it in her father's house. It was the same story she had found in Percy's desk, read, enjoyed, and triumphantly presented to him one day when he was feeling particularly depressed. "Why not turn this into a novel?" she had urged, thinking he had written the story. "It's perfect. It'll make a great mystery."

Her father had shrugged off the idea at the time, but a few days later he had presented her with a completed

outline for a new novel, using the story as the basis for
the plot. That had been the beginning. Several months
later she herself had finished the final draft of *An Intricate
Solution* as her father lay dying.

But how, *how* could such a mix-up have occurred?
~~Her father had obviously kept his copy~~ of the story Stephen
had given him to evaluate so long ago. He had forgotten,
apparently, that it was not his own creation. But was that
possible? Could one forget such a thing? Her father's
mental state had suffered as a result of his stroke, but
had he really been so confused?

He must have been. The only other possibility—that
Percy Quentin had known full well he had never written
the story—was too difficult for Viola to accept. Her
father would not knowingly have plagiarized Stephen's
material. He was an inventive writer, and an honest man.

Raising her head from her laced fingers, she looked
up at Stephen. He was standing quietly beside her, watching her with patient, weary eyes. He looked as if he felt
sorry for her.

Suddenly she was angry all over again. It wasn't fair
that he should have the power to destroy her father's
literary reputation! How could she have any sort of relationship with such a man? Damn him! She felt like
taking his short story and his article and ripping them
both to shreds.

She was silent for so long that Stephen took a shot
glass and a bottle of brandy from the bottom drawer of
his desk and poured her some. "Viola? Drink this, sweetheart."

His voice caressed her, and she felt a pang of grief
deep within her. She loved him. Their lovemaking had
been ecstasy, and all night long their personal communion had flowed freely and joyfully. It was true that they
had only just met each other again after eleven years,
yet everything had been so perfect, as if they'd known
each other all their lives. She was hooked; there was no
doubt about it. After only one night she was his.

But, being honest with herself, she was by no means

certain that he felt the same way. He had acted loving, but that didn't mean he loved her, or even considered her special. After all, he had avoided the commitment of a second marriage for eleven years.

Besides, she remembered ominously, he had warned her before making love that he regarded her as a casual weekend fling, and, to make it worse, he had just admitted that it had given him pleasure to strike a blow against her dead father through her.

"Listen, darling," he said, taking the shot glass away as soon as she had swallowed the burning liquid, "before you get all bent out of shape, you ought to know that I'm probably not going to publish that article."

"Why not?" When he didn't reply immediately, she raised her eyes questioningly. "Surely not because of what happened between us last night?"

The brief hope that had flared for an instant died as he shook his head. "No, not because of that. Sex in exchange for my silence—no."

She bristled. "You mean you set a higher price on your silence?"

His eyes narrowed. "Is that what you really think?"

"I don't know what to think. You tell me," she snapped.

He waved his hand impatiently over the papers on his desk. "Last night had nothing to do with any of this," he said angrily.

"To me it certainly didn't. Last night I didn't even *know* about any of this. You're the one with the grudge against my father, Stephen. You're the one who regards me as an instrument for your revenge."

"Don't be ridiculous, Viola." He took her chin between rough fingers and forced her head back so she had to meet his eyes. "Did I make love to you cold-bloodedly? Did I act as if I was motivated by anything other than pure, unadulterated desire?"

Pure, unadulterated desire. Not affection. Not love.

She tossed a short, harsh insult at him. His grip on her tightened.

"You're taking your disillusionment out on me," he

went on. "I warn you, I won't stand for it. I know you're
upset, but Percy's dead, dammit, and I'm alive and your
lover. You're going to have to let him go. His sins are
his own. Whether or not I publish that article ultimately
has nothing to do with you."

"You're wrong about that; it has everything to do with
me!" she cried, twisting her head, trying to free herself
from his punishing fingers. "You're hurting me," she
added.

The pressure let up, but he didn't let her go. His other
arm came around behind her shoulders and caressed the
back of her neck. In spite of everything, she felt a delicate
throb between her legs.

"Why?" he challenged. "What does it have to do with
you that Percy stole an idea from a former student of
his?"

She was going to have to tell him, she realized sickly.
She would confess her part in *An Intricate Solution*'s
creation, and his hatred would be redirected at her. The
warmth she could still see in his green eyes would fade
forever, and he would thrust her away from him in dis-
gust. She didn't want to tell him, but how could she
continue to let him lay all the blame at her father's door?

"Well?" he demanded impatiently.

"The whole thing's my fault. That's what it has to do
with me," she said wretchedly. "I found the story and
gave it to Daddy. I urged him to turn it into a novel. It
didn't have your name on it," she added defensively. "I
assumed it was an old manuscript of his."

When he didn't interrupt, she continued, "He was far
sicker after his stroke than anybody realized. He'd signed
a contract to do another novel and had accepted the ad-
vance, and I thought we were under obligation to his
publisher. Besides, he was depressed; he needed something to take his mind off his illness. I thought writing
another book would be good therapy for him, and his
doctors agreed.

"He resisted at first, but once he got going on the
project, it really did revive him. But then he got worse

and couldn't finish it." She looked up at him defiantly. "I wrote the last few pages and reworked the final draft. You're the only person I've ever admitted that to. Without me, there never would have been *An Intricate Solution*. It's all my doing, Stephen. You can throw me out now if it'll make you feel better!"

"Don't be an idiot!" he rejoined, matching her vehement tone. "What kind of twisted mind do you imagine me to have? Everything you've just told me only confirms my opinion of him—and of you. You loved him, you were loyal to him, and you gave up several months of your life to care for him after his stroke. I can't fault you for that, sweetheart. I only wish you weren't so thickheadedly blind to his real character."

"Nothing will make me believe he deliberately stole your idea," she said stubbornly. "He was far too decent and honorable a man to do such a thing."

Stephen's mouth twisted. "Decent and honorable," he repeated bitterly. "Listen to you! Is it really possible for a grown woman to be so stupid?" His voice roughened as he seemed to lose the control he'd been courting so determinedly. "I'll tell you how decent and honorable he was, Viola. The man had the morals of a back-alley tomcat. Believe me, stealing a story from me was nothing to him. He'd already stolen my wife." He flung the words at her. "Your precious father was the reason for my divorce."

"What?" she mouthed, her eyes round, her heart skipping.

He shook her, his finger biting into her shoulders. "Yes, Viola. I wasn't going to tell you. I didn't think, frankly, that it was any of your business. But as long as this has all come out, we may as well wallow in the whole sordid mess. Your father seduced my wife."

# CHAPTER
## *Eight*

"No," SAID VIOLA. She backed away from him. "I don't believe you."

"It's true," he insisted. "For a whole year before I met you, your father pretended to be interested in my writing, but all he was really after was Carol. He used to invite us both to dinner, charming her right under my nose. She fell for him, and a couple of months later, without explanation, she started divorce proceedings."

He stopped. She was staring distractedly out to sea, her heart thudding in her ears. It fit, she realized. Much as she wanted to deny everything she was hearing, it fit. It accounted for the breach between Stephen and her father, the years of silence, the still-flaring anger, the look on his face last night as he had briefly touched upon the breakup of his marriage.

"The affair went on, of course, after our separation, as did my cozy relationship with Percy," he continued.

"Idiot that I was, I never even suspected. I might never have discovered who Carol's lover was if it hadn't been for you."

Her eyes jerked back to meet his. "Me?"

"Yes." His voice was harsh. "Not long after that fateful weekend we both remember so well, Percy had a sudden urge to confess. He came to my place and told me that now that the divorce was final, he wanted everything to be open and aboveboard between us. He admitted that he was Carol's lover, and he even claimed that she had been there at the cottage that Saturday afternoon while you and I were out in the sailboat. He implied that you knew about their relationship—that he'd asked you to keep me busy so they wouldn't be disturbed."

He stopped again, his eyebrows raised in challenge.

"That isn't true!" His revelations seared her; she could hardly think. "Stephen, I was seventeen! How could I have done such a thing?"

"I realize that now, but then it seemed as though there wasn't a single human being on the face of the earth whom I could trust. I bought his story. It infuriated me. I could have killed him."

The violence in his voice sent a spiral of fear coiling through her. He looked as capable of murder as one of the villains in his books.

"I could have killed you."

She shivered, clasping her arms around herself, as Stephen continued. "I stopped writing letters to you and never tried to contact you again—which was, of course, exactly what Percy wanted. He knew I'd fallen for you, but it wouldn't have been very convenient, would it, for me to be mixed up with his daughter while he was making it with my ex-wife. Too messy. Percy liked things neat."

"Oh, no, Stephen, tell me this is only an unpleasant joke."

"It's no joke. Your father was a very clever man. He wanted to separate us, so he duped us both."

"The plagiarism thing we can straighten out, but this . . ."

"The plagiarism thing only came up a couple of months ago, after the publication of *An Intricate Solution.* I've hated Percy for years. He dumped Carol within a few months, of course, when the next foolish young woman came along. Literary gossip has it that Percy was never faithful to any woman for long."

She stared at him, stunned and disbelieving. But he was relentless. "Why in heaven's name do you suppose your mother left him? He was a skirt-chaser all his life."

"Stop it!" she cried. She had heard enough. Throwing him a look of agonized hostility, she turned and fled down the spiral staircase to the bedroom, then out into the hall and down to the living room. Jerking open the sliding doors, she ran across the deck and down the sand-coated steps to the beach. She had to get away. But she couldn't run from the voice in her mind that kept repeating every word Stephen had just said.

The sand was cold under her bare feet, and there was a sharp chill in the early morning air. She ran down to the edge of the water and stared out to sea. The waves made little sucking noises in the sand around her toes.

"He was a skirt-chaser all his life." Why did this revelation make her feel ill? She'd always thought her parents' divorce had been her mother's fault. But if what Stephen said was true . . . No, it couldn't be! Slowly, she forced herself to face what was probably the truth. Even she had noticed that her father had always been a bit of a charmer with the ladies.

For some reason she suddenly remembered Douglas. Her father had been unfaithful to her mother, and Douglas had been unfaithful to her. Douglas had been like her father in other ways, too, she realized for the first time. They were both controlling, domineering men who hid their true emotions behind a mask of gentlemanly politeness. A vivid memory rose into her conscious mind, making her tremble with its intensity: her father's face contorting as he screamed at her mother over some minor household failure, and his hand swinging back to strike her. "He hurt me deeply," Martha Quentin had said, after leaving the marriage. Until this moment Viola had never understood what her mother had meant.

Much agitated, she began to pace back and forth along the waterline, ignoring the chill of the sea, which numbed her ankles. She couldn't think about this now, she told herself, driving the unpleasant memories back into the dark corner of her mind where they had been hidden for so long. This was too much to deal with now. But the voice wouldn't stop.

As Stephen had said, she'd been blind. She had deceived herself about her father, and had repeated the self-deception in marrying Douglas. It had never struck her before that Douglas was so like her father. She had made the same mistake her mother had made.

She'd heard it said that women often fell in love with men who were similar to their fathers. She'd done it once, and now here she was again, getting herself mixed up with a mystery writer, of all people. Was she repeating the same insidious process? Was Stephen also a domineering brute who would eventually be unfaithful to her? Would she have fallen for him so easily if he had been an attorney or a truck driver?

What did she know, after all, of Stephen's real character? He was moody and changeable; he could be cruel; he could be charming. But what of his deeper qualities? Was he capable of commitment? For years she had given her love to two men who had been incapable of returning it—her father and Douglas. She had been foolish, perhaps, but at least she could love. Stephen had been divorced for over a decade, and he still resented his ex-wife. He was capable of holding a long-term grudge; that was certain. But was he capable of love?

It didn't matter, she realized miserably. If Stephen ever fell in love with anybody, it certainly wouldn't be with Viola Quentin, the daughter of his worst enemy. He had slept with her in retaliation for the wrong done him by her father. Revenge. Hardly a firm foundation on which to build a relationship.

"Dear God," she moaned, her brain in turmoil. She leaned over and scooped up some fragile pink shells from the beach, letting them fall back through her fingers to the wet sand. There was a small mound at her feet, which she dimly recognized as the remnants of the castle she and Stephen had built yesterday. It had been nudged by the tide, and nothing remained of the intricate design they had laughed and playfully argued over. It made her throat ache to see it.

She would have to leave. The sooner the better. Stephen didn't love her, would never love her. She remembered his hands, his mischievous grin, his low, sexy urgings, and grief knifed through the very core of her. It was like the last time, only far, far worse. Then she had been a child who hadn't really known what she wanted. Now she was a woman who had never met another man who could delight her on as many levels as Stephen could.

And she didn't just want him for a lover; she wanted to marry him. She wanted *this* mystery writer all for her own, forever. If that was crazy, so be it. She loved him.

Exerting all her willpower, Viola forced herself to stop thinking about how much she loved and needed Stephen. That road was a dead end. She might be crazy enough to fall in love overnight, but he certainly wasn't. She must turn around and crawl back to the grim fact that there was a big difference between fantasy and real life.

Reality was quick to intrude on her. She turned to see Stephen close the sliding door to the deck and walk down the steps toward her. He had donned a pair of jeans and a windbreaker. His hands were stuffed into his pockets, and his face was expressionless, but there was something almost lethal about the way he moved.

She turned back to the sea again without acknowledging him as he came up behind her. He placed one hand on her shoulder. "Viola?" he said simply.

"I'd like to be alone for a while."

"You've *been* alone for a while. It's cold out here. Come back to bed."

She stiffened. "No," she returned decisively, knowing instantly that this was the way it had to be. "That's over, Stephen."

The hand on her shoulder seemed to get heavier. "So that's what you've decided, have you?" he said in a low tone. "I tell you a few unpalatable truths and all of a sudden you don't want to have anything further to do with me?"

She turned reluctantly to face him. "What do you care?" she said bitterly. "You've had your revenge."

He stared at her with narrowed eyes. A gull cried over their heads, then swooped down over the quiet waves, seeking its prey. "You really think that?" he asked, searching her face.

"Yes. I don't know if it's conscious or unconscious, Stephen. Perhaps you don't care to admit to yourself that it was all you wanted me for. I'm not being critical. In a way, I understand. You loved Carol, and you must have felt horribly betrayed when she cheated on you. Maybe you're still in love with her; I don't know. But I do know that there's too much bitterness between your family and mine for there to be any hope for us. Too much damage has been done, Stephen."

When he didn't speak, she assumed he agreed with her. And that hurt. Trying to hide her pain, she went on, "Anyway, as we agreed, last night was just a casual affair. It's morning now, and I wish to end it the way I end all my casual affairs. I'm leaving. No doubt we'll both feel a lot more comfortable when I'm gone."

She tried to move away from him, but he held her with both hands gripping her upper arms. "You're not going anywhere," he said.

"Don't go all macho on me," she warned. "I'm not in the mood."

"I don't care what mood you're in," he said heatedly.

"If you think you can treat me the same way you treat 'all your casual affairs,' you're mistaken, Viola Quentin."

"My name is Bennett, not Quentin," she protested absurdly.

"Don't blame me for your lack of liberation!" he roared, his volatile anger blazing in his hard green eyes. "If you choose to call yourself by your sadistic husband's name instead of by your lecherous father's, it's all the same to me. Neither of them is around to claim you any longer. I am, and I do. We're going back to bed."

"Since I don't call myself by your name, you haven't the right," she retorted carelessly.

"Is that a proposal?" he shot back. "I accept."

"Don't be ridiculous," she gasped, pained to the quick that he could make a cruel joke about such a thing.

"What? You never consider marrying any of your casual affairs? Do you dump them all by the dawn's early light after you've beguiled them with your sweet body all night long? Do you give everything you have to all of them, responding so fully, making yourself so vulnerable? Do you laugh with all of them at the ultimate moment?"

"Yes!" she returned, furious. He actually believed that she indulged in casual affairs. "Yes to everything. What's the matter? Did you think you were special? Your ego is really magnificent, isn't it."

"My ego isn't easily undermined; that's certainly true," he told her in a milder tone. His fingers tilted her face up to his. "If your feelings for me are really so casual," he countered, "how come there are tears in your eyes?"

"Because I'm mad!" she shouted. "I get emotional when I'm mad."

"I like you when you're mad." His head came down, and he kissed her. Her hands pressed futilely against his shoulders as he crushed her against him, but almost instantly she felt her resistance slipping. She wanted nothing more than to sink against him and be borne up by his strength. But she couldn't, she reminded herself. It was brutal enough already, this struggle to tear herself away emotionally from the one man she wanted to love. But she had to protect herself. Somewhere inside him, she was sure, there was a man who hated her for being Percy Quentin's daughter.

So she fought him instead of yielding, there on the cold beach as the wind ripped at their clothes. She refused to give in to the tender pressure of his lips, or the persuasion of his tongue as it invaded the soft interior of her mouth. She tried to ignore the shivers generated by his hands moving over her tense body, molding her soft bottom, pulling her firmly against the hardness of him.

She managed to free her lips long enough to declare, "I don't want you, Stephen. Let go of me!"

"I don't care what you want," he growled. "You gave yourself freely to me last night, Viola. Over and over again. You belong to me now, and I won't stand politely aside while you attempt to deny it."

"Why not?" she demanded. "Do you want to make sure your revenge is total? Do you want me to fall madly in love with you all over again so you can subject me to the most refined tortures when you eventually reject me?"

"For a bright woman, you can be pretty thick sometimes," he muttered, taking her mouth again with almost savage insistence.

She had to get away from him, she thought, as desire fluttered deep in the pit of her stomach. One more minute of this and she'd be begging him to pleasure her with more of the rapturous lovemaking to which he had treated her all through the night.

She noticed the ruined sand castle just behind him, and, thinking of nothing but her need to escape, she took a step toward him, forcing him to step back. At the same moment she fondled the hair at the back of his neck and seemed to melt against him, so that he loosened his hold on her and whispered love words against her lips.

"I knew it," he crooned. "You can't pretend you don't want me, sweetheart."

She deliberately stumbled against him, forcing him

back another step, directly into the wet mound of sand. As he shifted slightly off balance, she gave him an unexpected shove, and he went down, flattening the ruined castle beneath the rugged weight of his body.

She turned and ran toward her car. She could hear him shouting at her, but she kept going, putting all the speed she could into her escape.

Darting a look over her shoulder, she saw that he wasn't even trying to catch her. He was kneeling where she had left him, studying the ground where he had fallen, paying no more attention to her than he paid to the sea gulls that arced in lazy circles over the waves.

An intense pain shot through her, making her realize that the foolishly passionate woman locked up inside her wanted nothing more than to be chased, captured, and hauled back to bed. But he was going to let her go. He was going to let her run out of his life without trying to stop her.

She wasn't looking where she was going, and she tripped over a clump of sand grass that rose out of the dune. Losing her balance, she fell heavily, her left foot twisting awkwardly beneath her as she went down. She felt a sharp pain in her ankle, and a cry escaped her.

This was the last straw. All the strength ran out of her. Flat on her stomach in the cold sand, she turned her face into a clump of grass and started to sob.

It seemed an age before she felt hard hands turning her over. The brief flow of tears had stopped. Stephen was kneeling over her, holding her shoulders down with the palms of his hands.

"You devil," he said unpleasantly. His legs straddled hers, and he lowered his head to kiss her sand-streaked face. His tongue drove into her mouth, and his jeaned hips ground against hers. "Have you got any more nasty little tricks to show me?"

"Get off me, Stephen," she said, her voice surprisingly calm.

He stayed where he was. "Just where did you think you were going?"

"To my car. Then home."

"You wouldn't have gone very far. Your keys are inside, in your purse."

"Stupid of me," she said sarcastically.

His mouth moved down her throat toward her breasts. "Very stupid. I don't like being physically abused. For that, I assure you, I *am* going to take my revenge."

She instantly detected the same lighthearted note with which he always tempered his dominant-male act, but this time it only made things worse. If he were as macho as he pretended to be, she'd find it easy to despise him, perhaps even to fear him, considering what Douglas had done to her. But after only one night in his bed, she had concluded that Stephen would never hurt her—physically, at least.

She turned her face aside as his mouth came down again. "No, Stephen," she said coldly. "I mean it. It's over between us. I'm going to go inside and get my keys and go home to Whittacre, and nothing you can say or do is going to stop me."

"We'll see about that," he said, rising so promptly to the challenge that she could have kicked herself for issuing it. He took her chin roughly between his thumb and forefinger and turned her face back to his. The other hand anchored her hair to the sand as he kissed her invasively, his tongue plunging deep into the warmth of her mouth. One of his muscular legs slid between hers, forcing them apart, and she gasped in pain as his foot pressed down on her injured ankle.

His head came up with a jerk. From the concern in his eyes, Viola could see that he had recognized her gasp as one of distress, not passion, and for the hundredth time, it seemed, she was startled by the power of their subliminal communication. Mentally they were attuned to each other, but verbally they were so often at odds!

"You're hurt?" He immediately lifted some of his weight off her. "I'm sorry . . . I didn't realize."

"I twisted my ankle when I fell. It—damn!" she cried, as he shifted and once again bumped the injured foot.

"Maybe it's broken," she added when she got her breath.

Stephen was more careful this time as he disentangled their bodies. Kneeling at her feet in the sand, he gently pushed up the material of her jeans to examine her left foot.

"It's swelling up, I'm afraid. Can you move your toes?"

Gritting her teeth against the pain, she tried to. Sweat blossomed on her forehead. "It really hurts," she said, somewhat surprised. Before he'd knocked against it, all she'd felt was a dull ache. Now her entire foot was alive with pain.

"That's enough," he ordered sharply, as she shifted her toes slightly. "Let's not make it worse. It's either broken or sprained. Whichever, you're going to have to keep off it for a while." He shot her a leer. "You'll just have to stay in my bed until it's well enough for you to walk. That'll teach you to run away from me," he added, eyebrows raised wickedly.

"Don't be ridiculous. I've got classes tomorrow. Damn. I'll need crutches." She spoke calmly, but she was feeling considerable dismay. If she couldn't walk, she couldn't get her keys and leave, and if she couldn't leave immediately . . . if she slept with him again . . .

"Right now you need a good soak and a bandage. Later, an X ray, I think. Come on, darling. Let's get you inside."

Once again he lifted her in his arms, carefully cradling her injured leg as he marched back over the dunes to the house.

"You're so strong," she murmured sardonically, her lips against his throat. She was making a valiant effort to laugh instead of cry. "More powerful than a locomotive, able to leap tall buildings in a single bound."

He smiled easily at her, making her feel almost as if the unpleasantness of the past hour had been a dream. "Actually, you weigh a ton," he said ungraciously.

"Don't hurt yourself, Stephen, please. I can walk, or, rather, hop."

But he shook his head and continued to stride up the path to the house. Once through the sliding door to the living room, she expected him to put her down on the nearest couch, but instead he mounted the stairs to the bedroom. "Don't worry. I work out several times a week at the Nautilus Club. Where do you suppose I get my magnificent physique?"

He laid her down carefully on the water bed. Just the feel of it warmly supporting her ankle helped to diminish the pain. She closed her eyes thankfully, wishing she could stay here forever, in his room, in his bed, with the ocean stretched out before her and the sea-feel of his luxurious mattress soothing her weary limbs.

"Better?"

She nodded.

"Rest. I'm going to get something to soak your foot in, and an aspirin or two."

Viola obeyed. She couldn't think anymore anyway. The revelations of the dawn, coming hard upon the ecstasies of the night, had flooded her mind to a point where she felt dull and sluggish. In a way she was almost grateful for the pain in her foot, since it occupied all her attention. She focused on the pain and let everything else go blank.

When Stephen came back with bandages, a basin of water, and towels, the first thing Viola noticed was that he had taken off the windbreaker and was, once again, bare-chested. Through half-closed lashes, she surveyed the wealth of black, crinkly hair springing from his strong chest and tracking down in a glossy ribbon into the waistband of his low-slung jeans. She wanted to follow its path and touch him intimately, feel him spring to life beneath her teasing fingers as he had done so astonishingly often during the night. His green eyes captured hers, and she blushed.

"Yes," he said solemnly. "I agree."

"You agree with what?" she demanded, even more embarrassed.

"With whatever you're thinking, moon goddess. Here,

take these." His voice became businesslike once more as he handed her two aspirin-substitute tablets and a glass of water. After she swallowed the pills, he put the basin down on the floor and bent over her to roll up the left leg of her jeans, touching her exceedingly gently. "Too tight," he said. His hands slid quickly up to her waist and found the snap and the zipper. "They'll have to come off."

"No," she protested, even as his fingers swiftly unfastened her.

"Give me some credit for civility," he returned, sounding slightly irritated. "I'm not going to force myself on your defenseless body while you're lying there with a broken ankle."

After that she didn't argue. She let him slide the blue jeans off her, and then the sweat shirt, because the sun was beginning to slant into the room and she was warm. She lay there nude while Stephen carefully draped her left leg down over the end of the bed and into the basin of cold water. After a while he applied cold compresses instead. When the swelling seemed to have stopped, he dried her foot and wrapped her ankle in a bandage.

"You missed your calling," she murmured as he completed his task. "You ought to have been a doctor."

"When I was a kid, I dreamed of being a vet. I used to run about searching for injured animals so I could nurse them back to health."

"Did you ever find any?"

"There was a bird once, a pigeon. Oscar, I named him. Something had gotten him—a cat maybe. He was badly gouged, and one wing was torn. I made a splint for his wing and rushed to the library to read bird books to find out what to feed him while he was convalescing." His voice had gone curiously soft, and his eyes were full of a young boy's pain.

"What happened to him?" she asked, already sure of the answer.

"He died."

She said nothing, but Stephen wasted no time in breaking the somber mood by adding lightly, "I certainly hope I have better luck with you."

"I hope so, too!"

"I like birds," he said after a silence. "You can see a lot of unusual ones down here if you know what to look for."

"You're into bird-watching?"

"In a very amateur sense. I don't know as much as I'd like to know."

"Birds," she repeated dreamily. "You don't like people much, do you? You live alone out here, plying your isolated trade, watching birds and writing about your misanthropic hero—"

"I thought he was misogynistic?"

"He's both; he hates women *and* men."

"I don't hate anybody," said Stephen.

Except Percy, Viola thought. And me. "No," she agreed bitterly. "You're sweet and gentle and loving— not at all like Max. He certainly wouldn't tend the ankle of a woman who'd shoved him into a sand pile, would he? He'd probably shoot her for it, being careful not to get any blood on his expensive three-piece suit."

Stephen nodded gravely. "He would undoubtedly shoot her." He clipped the end of the bandage into place and slid up beside her on the bed. He still wore only his blue jeans, which somehow lent him a rakish air. She had a brief vision of him as a sixteenth-century pirate, and of herself lying naked and helpless beside him, the captive he intended to ravish.

His wiry pelt of chest hair was close to her face as he stretched out at her right side, away from the sprain, and propped himself up on one elbow. He swayed a little with the waves. His eyes gazed intently down into hers as he said, "How're you feeling?"

She reached out and smoothed her fingers through the rough hair on his chest, reveling in the way it curled around her fingertips, imprisoning them. There was a sharp pull inside her. She tried to ignore it. She told herself firmly that she must ignore it.

"The pain's much less now, thanks to you," she answered. Tearing her eyes away from his body, she added, "I think I'm fading. I'm really very tired."

"I'll help you relax," he said agreeably. "Turn over. I'll rub your back."

"No, Stephen, I—"

"Don't argue with the doctor, love." He gently rolled her over, careful not to jar her ankle, then knelt over her and began to massage the tense muscles in her neck and shoulders. His strokes were firm and professional, not overtly sensual, and she felt her stiffness ease. With the heels of his hands he smoothed and pounded her muscles, and the bed undulated beneath them in rhythm with his movements.

"Stephen, about my father—" she began.

"No," he interrupted harshly, "not now. Your instinct last night was the right one: when we're in bed together it's you and me. There's no room for thoughts of anyone else."

As if to emphasize this, he spread his thighs to kneel astride her bottom, a position that put him more fully in control. The rough denim of his jeans against her naked flesh reminded her of her fantasy of being his willing captive, and her body flashed instantly from relaxation to arousal.

His hands slid from her shoulders to her thighs, still stroking with a driving force that pressed her deep into the water bed, then moved back up along her spine. His fingers trailed along her sides as the heels of his hands applied the pressure, and when they reached her rib cage, she could feel his fingertips teasing the sides of her breasts.

A soft, throaty sound was wrung from her as his hands danced delicately over her upper back. He gathered up her thick skein of hair and spread it up over her head to expose the sensitive nape of her neck to his clever, tantalizing fingers. His head came down, and his tongue explored her ear and the side of her throat. She couldn't contain her moans of pleasure.

Lifting her upper body slightly, he reached under to

find her breasts, which filled his hands. He tugged gently on the nipples, making her shudder with desire. She forgot about Percy and Douglas and *An Intricate Solution*. She forgot how desolate she was going to feel when she was banished—as she was bound to be—from his bed. She even forgot the pain in her ankle.

With some difficulty, she rolled onto her back. He remained astride her, massaging the front of her body with the same long, deep strokes he had used on her back. She squirmed when his hands traveled over her breasts, flattening them momentarily before his fingers went to work to bring the nipples out again in hard, tingling points.

"You're beautiful," he whispered, his eyes paying tribute to her glowing, undulating nakedness. He added a blatantly sexual description of what he wanted to do to her, and she smiled, silently inviting him to go ahead and do it.

"How's your foot?"

"Who cares? Some massage, Doctor." Her fingers went to the waistband of his blue jeans and unfastened them. "I want you."

"I'm afraid of hurting you."

"You won't hurt me."

"I promise I'll let you go to sleep right afterward," he said contritely, cautiously lifting himself off her to undress. When he came back his fingers checked her and found her ready. "Sexy lady," he whispered huskily.

Supporting himself on his hands and knees, he surged against her and entered with a long, slow thrust. At the same time his head came down and he took one of her nipples in his mouth and sucked it hard, then nipped it with his teeth. She cried out in pleasure, rocking beneath him and thrusting back with all the force in her body. They went on like that, slowly, deliciously, for many long minutes, until both of them were sweating and gasping and the bed was rolling with the waves of their passionate striving.

Afterward, Viola snuggled spoon-fashion in his arms,

the long lines of his body coiled around her back and legs and shoulders. She closed her eyes contentedly and murmured, "I knew it. I'm in bed with Superman. How can I resist the man of steel?"

His laugh was warm and affectionate. "Idiot," he retorted. "Go to sleep."

"You're so masterful," she sighed, and obeyed.

# CHAPTER
## *Nine*

WHEN VIOLA AWOKE several hours later, she stretched and rolled over, seeking the warm body that had cradled her, making her feel as warm and safe as a child. As she moved, two things flashed into her consciousness: first, that her ankle hurt, and second, that she was alone.

She opened her eyes. Sunshine was streaming into the room, and the clock read eleven-fifteen. Stephen was gone. His clothes had been removed from the floor. She wondered how long he'd been up.

She pushed herself to a sitting position, trying not to jar her ankle. "Stephen?" she called out softly. There was no reply. She listened for the sound of his typewriter, but the house was quiet. He must be downstairs, or maybe out running on the beach.

She leaned back against the pillows and with her fingers tentatively examined her injured ankle. It was still swollen and tender to the touch. She certainly wouldn't be able to walk today. Fortunately it was her left leg, or she wouldn't be able to drive herself home. Not that she wanted to go home, she thought, remembering their love-making. But she had classes tomorrow.

For several minutes she allowed herself to relive the passionate engagements of Stephen's body with her own, the love passages that had taken place here on the warm and flowing water bed throughout the night. But when she caught herself fantasizing about the next time, and how wonderful it would be, she firmly ordered herself back down to earth.

There wouldn't be a next time. Nothing had changed. Stephen was tender and sexy, but he had said nothing about loving her, nothing about caring, nothing about ever seeing her again. The sooner she accepted it, the better for both of them. It was Sunday, and their casual weekend affair was over.

Glancing again at the clock, Viola noticed a folded piece of paper propped up against the table lamp. She was certain it hadn't been there earlier. She reached over and grabbed it.

"Sweetheart," the note began, "You look so peaceful sleeping there that I don't have the heart to wake you. I have to take a quick ride to Provincetown to appear at a book fair—publicity, you know. I promised my publisher I'd do it. I meant to take you along, but I think you'd better have a rest instead. I'll be back in a couple of hours, and we can get you to the doctor to have that ankle of yours X-rayed."

He had skipped a space, then added, in capital letters, "You were beautiful, Professor." Under this, he had scrawled his name. At the top of the note, the time was written: 11:00 A.M. He must have just left.

Viola folded the note, trying to stifle her disappointment at his absence. This was the best thing that could have happened, she told herself impatiently. While he was gone, she would leave.

He was dangerous, she reminded herself. Already he had possessed her body and hollowed out a place for himself in her heart. But there was still a part of her he hadn't penetrated. The locked up core of her was still protected, unravished, safe. If stripping her entirely bare and then discarding her was his vengeful intent, he hadn't quite succeeded—yet.

The rational part of her mind told her that this melo-dramatic assessment of Stephen's intentions was way off base, that he simply wasn't so Machiavellian. But the emotional part of her—the generous, loving heart that had met with hurt and rejection from one too many men—refused to trust Stephen. It was this side of her that opened his note again and peered at the signature. Not "Love, Stephen." Not "Fondly, Stephen." Just "Stephen."

She rolled the note up into a ball and threw it to the floor.

Ten minutes later, Viola was hobbling out onto the deck at the back of the house, fumbling in her handbag for her car keys. The sun was glaring on the sand in the driveway, sending flashes and gleams sparkling off the chrome of—Stephen's racy BMW. She stared, one hand still in her bag and the other clutching at the railing. Stephen's car was indeed parked there, its hood raised, signaling its stubborn refusal to start. But next to it, where her own car had been parked, there was an empty space.

No wonder she hadn't been able to find her keys! Stephen had taken her car to Provincetown, the artists' colony at the tip of the Cape, leaving her stranded. He had effectively made a prisoner of her.

Viola carefully sat down on the top step. Her heart was beating in that crazy staccato way that was getting to be habitual.

How dare he take her car without asking her? How dare he take her calm and peaceful life into his hands and wrench it until she didn't know what she really wanted? The image of his naked body leaning over hers came into her mind with the clarity of a vision. She had to get out of here.

She dragged herself down the steps to the driveway.

Maybe she could start his car. She had once taken a course in auto mechanics. She opened the door and looked in at the ignition. There were no keys, of course—he must have taken them with him. Never mind, she didn't need keys. With grim pleasure she remembered the professional car thief she'd interviewed one summer in grad school when she'd written the free-lance article on stolen vehicles. He'd taught her a trick or two that she hadn't forgotten.

Viola looked under the hood. It took only about two minutes to find the problem. The main cable to the distributor cap was disconnected. She plugged it back in and set about hot-wiring the ignition. When she finally touched the proper wires together, the engine roared into action.

It wasn't until she had installed herself in the comfortable leather driver's seat that it came to her that either Stephen was a total idiot when it came to cars, or he had disconnected the cable himself.

But why? she asked herself. Why would he deliberately disable his car? His claim that something was wrong with the engine—had that been a lie from the start? He'd been about to drive to her house late Friday night when he'd called her back to say his car wouldn't start. Had he suddenly decided he was too tired to make the trip and used the car as an excuse? Or had he wanted to trap her into coming down here, to his turf, where he'd be able to exert all his considerable powers to seduce her—with a gourmet dinner, a romantic stroll on the beach, moonlight, and a water bed?

The more she thought about it, the angrier she got. He had set up this weekend from beginning to end. He had seduced her last night, seduced her again this morning when she'd been determined to leave, and now he was trying to have his cake and eat it too by going off to a book fair to sell more copies of his damn book while making certain she wouldn't be able to take off in his absence. It had never occurred to him, no doubt, that she knew anything about cars. Had he really expected to trick her with so elementary a ploy? Arrogant, self-confident beast!

There was only one problem, she realized, when she tried to put the BMW into gear. The car had a standard transmission, and it hurt her ankle terribly when she pressed down on the clutch. Still, she'd have to grit her teeth and bear it. Once she got out on the highway she wouldn't have to shift, and things wouldn't be so bad.

They would still have to meet to exchange cars, but she'd worry about that later. Nothing mattered now beyond getting away from the place where Stephen Silkwood had taken her body and made it his own—stealing more than a little of her soul in the process. With one last look at the curve of the shining sea licking the white sands, she reversed gears and made her escape.

Two hours later, when she finally reached her house back in Whittacre, Viola hopped inside and found her telephone ringing stridently. She stared at it for a moment, then steeled herself to answer. It couldn't be Stephen. He was probably still at his damn book fair.

"Hello?"

She heard someone draw a long breath at the other end.

"Stephen?" she said tentatively.

"Words fail me," the familiar voice returned. He slammed down the phone.

She closed her eyes and sank into a chair. She knew what he was going to do as surely as if they shared the same brain. What good had it done to run from him? As long as he desired her, he wouldn't let her go. He was strong-willed, stubborn, passionate. And he liked to be in control. There was more of Max Trencher in him than he would admit.

Well, she could be stubborn, too. She, too, had strength, guts, and determination. She was not going to cave in like a house of cards. If he wanted her, let him make a serious commitment to her. If all he wanted was a few nights of pleasure, let him find another partner.

The phone rang again. This time she grabbed it on the first ring and shouted into the receiver, "Stop calling me, damn you! All I want is for you to leave me alone!"

"Viola?" The voice, which was not Stephen's this time, sounded extremely taken aback. "This is David Newstead," he added uncomfortably.

"David!" she gasped. "Good heavens, I'm sorry. I thought it was someone else." There was an uneasy silence; then she quickly added, "How are you?"

"I'm fine, how are you?"

"Fine. Well, not so fine, actually," she admitted ruefully. "You must think I'm very rude."

"No," he assured her. "I just called to see how you were. I've called you several times this weekend, but there was no answer. You seemed kind of down the other night at the concert."

The other night seemed eons ago. So much had happened since then. "That's very thoughtful of you, David," she said gently.

"I just wanted to repeat," he went on, "that if you ever need a friend, or someone to talk to...I know you haven't been living here very long, and you probably don't know many people in town, and, well, I like you, Viola. As a friend," he added hurriedly, as if fearful of being too forward.

Viola was moved. Why was it, she wondered, that she wasn't the least bit attracted to this man who was so thoughtful and kind? Why did she prefer to get mixed up with Stephen, who had probably never experienced a shy or awkward moment in his entire life?

"Listen, David," she said on impulse, "if you really mean it, there *is* something you can do for me."

"Of course," he said eagerly. "What?"

"I need a ride to the hospital. I've sprained my ankle, maybe broken it."

"Oh, Viola, I'll be right over. Don't try to walk. Just take it easy. I'll be there in a few minutes."

David was as good as his word. In ten minutes he

was at her doorstep, his expression one of deep concern.
He was dressed more casually than she had ever seen
him, in jeans and a sweater, and he actually looked quite
handsome with his wavy brown hair, pleasant features,
and sympathetic eyes.

"Viola! What happened? Does it hurt very badly?" He
took hold of her arm and helped her out to his car. "How
did you do it?"

"It's a long story," she said, knowing no easy way to
explain.

He helped her into the passenger seat and ran around
to get into the driver's side. She was glad she didn't have
to drive any farther herself. The shifting had been brutal.

"Did you get a new car?" David asked as he backed
around Stephen's sporty BMW.

"No, it belongs to a friend," she replied uneasily. She
didn't know what she was going to tell David about
Stephen. Guiltily, she realized that she must have been
temporarily insane when she'd asked for David's help.
They'd probably get stuck at the hospital, and by the
time they drove home, Stephen would undoubtedly be
there. How had her life suddenly become so complicated?

David cast her a worried glance as he drove, much
faster than was his wont, in the direction of the Whittacre
Community Hospital. "Viola, what's wrong? Something's bothering you, isn't it? Something besides your
ankle?"

What was with these mind-reading men? Was she
really so transparent? "It's nothing," she said.

"Please tell me."

His gentle voice cut through her defenses. Some defenses, she thought wryly. Stephen had made the breach;
now the entire bastion was beginning to crumble.

"It's an awkward situation," she began. "I don't want
to take advantage of your generosity, really. I shouldn't
have imposed on you."

"I'm tougher than I look. Just tell me." His brown
eyes were sincere. "It's got something to do with the guy

who owns the BMW, doesn't it?"

She nodded wearily. "The car belongs to the man with whom I"—she paused, then drew a quick breath and finished—"spent the night. He lives on the Cape. I was running on the beach this morning, and I fell and hurt my ankle. He'd taken my car for a couple of hours, thinking his own wouldn't start, but I managed to get it going, and I drove home. That's why I have his car and he has mine."

David's lips were tight, and his eyes stayed doggedly on the road. "You drove all the way up from the Cape with that ankle?"

"Yes, and I probably could have driven myself to the hospital, too. I shouldn't have asked you, David."

"Stop saying that. Why was it so imperative that you get away from this guy? You could have gone to a hospital there."

"I didn't want to see him again."

David looked angry now. "Was he responsible for your accident?"

She was startled. "Heavens, no, nothing like that." She paused, then added, "Look, I'll try to explain. The man is an old friend of mine, whom I just met again after a long separation. Out of nostalgia I agreed to see him yesterday, but it was a mistake. I don't want to get mixed up with him again."

David shot her a glance. She flushed and looked out the window. "He's very persistent," she continued more calmly. "He's going to be annoyed that I left, that I took his car. He'll probably come after me." She looked at David miserably. "He may even be there when we get back from the hospital."

"I see," said David in a neutral tone. His lips were still pressed together.

"You're angry."

"Yes," he confirmed. "At your persistent friend."

"If you drop me at the hospital, I'll take a taxi home."

"Viola, are you crazy?" He was smiling now and

looking quite pleased with himself. "You want me to make it clear to Romeo that you don't want anything more to do with him? I'd be delighted."

Viola stared. David was turning into a tiger before her very eyes. Is this what she had subconsciously wanted? A man at her side to protect her from Stephen? "I'll make it clear to him," she answered carefully. "But I guess I wouldn't mind a little support, if that's what you're offering."

"When it comes to support, I'm your man. You were right to call on me."

He sounded as if he meant it, and Viola was relieved that she wouldn't have to face Stephen alone.

The hospital was just around the corner, and as David lurched into the emergency room parking lot she smiled and said, "I think you set a record. It's probably only a sprain."

He came around to help her out of the car. "What are friends for?"

As she'd suspected, the ankle was badly sprained but not broken. Still, with the wait in the emergency room and later in the X-ray department, it was more than two hours before David was able to drive her, complete with her rented crutches, back to her house. He had kept the conversation on pleasant subjects the entire time they were together, for which Viola was grateful. But despite his efforts, she hadn't been able to put Stephen out of her mind.

It was an odd feeling—as if Stephen were with her. She seemed to feel the power of his emotions impinging on her consciousness constantly, as if a telepathic bond existed between them. She knew he was angry, and she knew he wasn't going to give up. So she wasn't surprised when they turned into the long driveway leading to her house and saw her car parked there beside his. He had come, as she had known he would.

"There's something I didn't tell you."

David turned to look at her. He seemed much calmer than she would have expected; she had always believed him to be the nervous type. So much for her perceptiveness about people, she told herself.

"You know this man," she went on. "You met him the other night at the college."

David looked blank. "I did?"

"He's Stephen Silkwood."

Now David did look nervous. "What? Stephen Silkwood is an old boyfriend of yours?"

"He told you he knew my father," she confirmed. "He also knew me, although he didn't recognize me at first."

"How could he not recognize you if—"

"It was a long time ago," she interrupted.

David pulled up and parked. There was no sign of Stephen. He must be waiting inside the house.

"Percy Quentin was your father, and Stephen Silkwood was your . . . ?"

She made a face. "I can't seem to get away from mystery writers, can I."

His eyes considered her seriously. "Are you certain you want to?"

"Yes, I'm positive." She met his gaze unflinchingly. "Do you want to leave?"

"No."

"He's not an easy man to deal with. He'll undoubtedly be rude. He may even go to rather melodramatic extremes."

"Maxwell Trencher in the flesh?"

"No, he's not dangerous. At least I don't think he is."

David sighed. "I'm not exactly a knight in shining armor."

"You'll do," she assured him, smiling.

Stephen was not in the hallway or the living room. He didn't answer when she called his name. "Maybe he just dropped the car here and took off," David suggested.

"No. He's here. I can feel it." And suddenly she knew where she'd find him.

She clattered down the hall toward the bedroom, still trying to get the hang of the crutches. David walked beside her, looking more curious than apprehensive. She felt a definite warmth for him. There weren't many people who'd willingly get involved in something this messy.

They found Stephen stretched out in the middle of her brass bed, a stack of papers at his side, one of which he was perusing with interest. The desk on the far side of the room had been rifled; there were books and papers everywhere. He raised his eyes to her as she paused on the threshold, giving her a slow smile.

"You did contribute to it, didn't you?" he said lazily. "I've found the working manuscript—cross-outs, rewrites, and all. I'm impressed. It looks as if you made a significant number of changes. I'll have to change the thrust of my article: Percy Quentin's daughter, Ph.D., accomplice in fraud."

Whatever she had expected, it was not this. The last thing she wanted David Newstead exposed to was the unfortunate story of the creation of *An Intricate Solution*. "You've no right to go through my private papers!" she cried.

"You started it, darling." His eyes narrowed as he noticed David, who had pushed into the room at Viola's outcry. He sat up and laid the papers aside. "Who's this? Your bodyguard?"

"My friend," she said stiffly. "David Newstead. I believe the two of you met the other night. David has just taken me to the hospital."

"What for? You can drive."

"Viola's ankle is badly sprained," David said angrily. "Don't you care?"

Stephen considered him with cold eyes. "Not particularly," he announced. "Viola is a very capable woman. Formidable, in fact. There's nothing she can't do. She teaches Shakespeare, she writes devastating book reviews, she hot-wires cars, and she's spectacular in bed—

but you know all that, of course. Don't you love the way she laughs right at the end, as if she's just discovered a hitherto unapprehended joy?"

He was furious, Viola realized. Not even that first evening at her house, when he'd discovered her identity, had he been so angry. He was looking at David as if he could barely keep himself from leaping up and strangling him.

"I think Viola wants you to leave," David said, none too steadily.

"Oh, come now," Stephen returned in a voice that shook with tautly leashed hostility, "there's room here for three." He patted the mattress beside him. "I'm perfectly willing to share her with you. And with any other of her 'casual affairs,' for that matter. We can't both expect to keep a sweet, smart, sexy lady like Viola all to ourselves, can we . . . what was your name again? David? Yes, I believe you were one of the ones she called out for in her sleep last night. Or was it Michael? Or Hugh? Or Tom, Dick, or Harry?"

"Stop it, Stephen," Viola said in a low, harsh voice. "Just stop it!"

His raging green eyes turned their full attention to her. "Get rid of him, Viola. Get rid of him, or I swear—"

"What?" she challenged. "What's the threat, exactly, Stephen? Or should I call you Max?"

He made a visible effort to control himself, stung, it seemed, by being identified with his fictional character. "What the hell induced you to take off like that?" he demanded. "I was home before one o'clock. I hurried back, impatient to see you again, having been rude as hell to everybody at the book fair. How could you do that to me? I was worried about you!"

"You disabled your car on purpose," she accused him. "You disconnected the distributor cable to make sure I wouldn't leave."

"I always disconnect it at night, ever since my last car got stolen out from under my nose," he shot back.

"You told me it wouldn't start," she sputtered.

"It wouldn't—Friday night. I had it fixed yesterday morning before you arrived. It needed a new battery. You're paranoid, Viola. What did you think I was doing, holding you prisoner?"

"Why did you take my car, then?"

"Because I've got about thirty unpaid traffic tickets registered in Provincetown against my license number, and I didn't feel like getting towed."

"Oh, come on. I don't believe you. You wanted to make sure I couldn't leave. You didn't think I knew about distributor cables."

He rose abruptly from the bed, uncoiling his long, tough body and straightening to his full height. He came very slowly and deliberately toward her, stopping maybe two feet away. "All right," he agreed, "I didn't think you knew about distributor cables. I certainly didn't think you knew how to bypass the ignition, nor did I think you could have driven very far with that ankle. I was afraid you'd wake up and decide to leave, so I tried to forestall you by taking your car. But I ought to have known that your ingenuity would be a match for any obstacle I put in your way. If I'd had any sense, I would have called the book fair organizers and canceled. Next time I won't be stupid enough to underestimate you, Professor."

"There's not going to be a next time," she said softly, wishing he wouldn't stand so close. Because of the awkwardness of her crutches, she couldn't even retreat. The proximity of his strong, tension-taut body made her feel weak with the renewed ache of desire. If it weren't for David's steady but equally tense presence at her side, she knew she wouldn't be able to resist the unspoken call of Stephen's body to hers.

"No?" he queried, even more softly. He ignored David and looked only at her. "That's where you're wrong, Viola."

"The weekend is over," she said firmly.

"So what? What's going to happen between you and me, love, has just barely begun."

His voice was outrageously seductive, and Viola's

blood roared with her heady reaction to his magnetism. Her tongue was too thick to answer, but David was not so mesmerized.

"I think you'd better leave now, Mr. Silkwood," he said.

Stephen didn't even glance at him. "I want you, Viola," he murmured huskily, "and I know you want me. You may think you can fight that, but you're going to find you can't."

"What I want is for you to get out of my house and out of my life!" she cried. "It's over. I won't allow you to tear my heart and soul to pieces all over again!"

"Oh, is that it, then? You're afraid to feel, Professor? What the hell were you doing last night—faking? You can't run away from your passions, darling, or haven't you learned that yet?"

Passions. It was always passions with him. Or unadulterated desire. The word *love* didn't exist for him. "I need more than passions, Stephen," she insisted. "I could experience those with any man."

This sparked his fury again. "Yes, I know. We've already established that—you and your casual affairs." He glared briefly at David, then looked back at her. "Still, what we have between us is not casual. Your heart was in it. I know it; I saw it in your eyes. You love me, Viola. You can't deny it."

She stared at him in horror, hearing him use the word *love* as if he'd extracted it directly from her dazed thoughts. How could he know the extent of her feelings for him? She'd been cool, sophisticated, thoroughly liberated, and modern, not at all like the seventeen-year-old who'd been incapable of hiding her bedazzlement. Only this morning, when she'd found out about the bitter complications between Stephen and her father had she revealed her deeper emotions. But surely not even then had she done anything to convince him that his revenge was going to be complete.

But no, she told herself, it was *not* going to be complete. He was not going to break her as Douglas had— never, never would she allow any man to do that to her again. There was still a part of her that he could not touch.

"I do deny it," she said firmly. Desperately, without thinking, she turned to David. "Do I look as if my heart is in my eyes every time you and I make love?" she whispered.

David flushed, staring at her lips. He bit his own, and in that moment Viola realized, with sudden, sick regret, that David desired her just as much as Stephen did, and that this entire conversation had been torture for him. Pain shot through her—hers, his, Stephen's; she couldn't tell them apart. She only knew that everything she had said and done until now had been justifiable, but this last outrageous question had not.

She started to say she was sorry, but before the words were out David stepped forward to enclose her, crutches and all, in his arms. He bent his head and kissed her lips.

"Yes, Viola," he said, "always."

Stephen turned without a word and left them alone.

Viola and David separated as soon as they heard the front door slam. Viola was trembling. "Oh, David," she said brokenly, "forgive me. I don't know what came over me. That was a despicable thing to do to you. I'm so sorry."

"You do love him, don't you," he said harshly.

She nodded.

David sat down unsteadily on the edge of the bed. "I think I need a drink," he said, trying to smile.

Viola hobbled off on her crutches to get him one, seizing the excuse to have a moment or two alone. She made her way to the living room, where the whiskey decanter was. From the front window she saw that Stephen had not yet left. He was outside, leaning with both hands braced against the roof of his car.

As she looked out the window, Stephen turned, and

once again Viola felt an odd sense of telepathic communion. An instant later he was striding back up the steps to the front door.

She was paralyzed. She couldn't breathe as the door opened and he faced her, grief and anger molding the contours of his handsome features.

"It was either leave or kill him."

"Stephen . . ."

"I'm not giving up, darling. I never give up. Without adopting Max's tactics, I can't stop you from sleeping with him or with any of your other casual boyfriends. But I have tactics of my own, and I'll employ them, I warn you, no matter how long it takes. You're going to be mine, and mine exclusively. You're going to declare your love for me and beg me—yes, plead with me—to do the same. You're going to learn what it means to be stalked, and how it feels to know that no matter how far away you run, there is no escape. Do you understand?"

As she stared at him, speechless, he bent his dark head and kissed her on the mouth. Then he turned without another word and walked down the porch steps, got into his car, and drove away.

Viola mixed David a Scotch and water, and poured a Scotch without a single drop of water for herself. But she knew it was going to take a good deal more than alcohol to make her forget Stephen's words.

# CHAPTER
## *Ten*

FOR THE NEXT few days, Stephen very cleverly manipulated Viola's emotions. Every morning she drove to class and tried to maintain some semblance of normalcy in front of her students and among her colleagues, but with her return home in the late afternoon, the careening roller coaster ride would crank up again. He was fulfilling his threat. And, as he had promised, it was not Max's style he was employing, but his own, and his own was full of surprises.

The biggest surprise was that he made no attempt to see her. She had steeled herself for the probability of having to repel his physical advances, wondering how on earth she would ever keep her resolve if he pressed her. But he didn't press her. He walked out on Sunday afternoon, and he didn't come back.

He began with a series of romantic gestures. When she arrived home from school on Monday, she found a box of long-stemmed red roses at her door, with a card that read, "To my casual weekend love, from your constant, daily lover." The next day flowers were delivered to her office at school, provoking much comment. When she got home, she received a special-delivery envelope containing a sonnet—competently written with the correct rhyme scheme—on her beauty. No one had ever written her a poem before. When she got to the couplet at the end, she astonished herself by bursting into tears.

Every night at midnight Stephen telephoned her, asking invariably, until she was ready to punch him, "Are you alone?" Their conversations ranged from strained to uninhibited. The first night they argued about the turning point in *Hamlet*, which she was teaching that week, until two in the morning. The second night he told her, his disembodied voice drifting seductively into her consciousness, exactly what he was going to do to her the next time he got her into bed, making her so hot and restless that she couldn't sleep until dawn. The third night she haltingly told him about the telephone conversation she had had that day with her mother.

"All these years I've thought it was her fault that she and my father got a divorce," she explained. "She left him, after all, and remarried again so soon. I asked her, for the first time, what really happened—was it true about the other women? She confirmed it, Stephen. For years she had blamed herself, thinking she must be sexually inadequate or something. It had taken months of therapy—and the reassuring love of her second husband—to convince her that such was not the case." Viola paused, her hand tightly clutching the telephone.

"Go on," Stephen said gently. "I'm listening."

"It was the first time I'd ever talked to my mother honestly, woman to woman. I told her about my own marriage, how Douglas had cheated on me and hurt me. We cried together, Stephen. It was"—she hesitated, at a loss for the right adjective—"nice," she finished, inadequately.

"I understand," he said. There was a long silence before he added, "Can I come up?"

He always asked it; she always refused. This time she almost broke down. "No," she managed to say.

"I started you agonizing about your parents. I want to be with you. I won't touch you if you're going to be so adamant about it."

"You couldn't keep that promise."

"No, probably not. Viola, why are you doing this to us? Sooner or later you know damn well you're going to sleep with me again. Why not give in and let it happen? What do I have to do, drag you off by the hair?" His voice dropped a register into its sexiest mode. "I will if you don't break down soon. I'll unleash Max on you."

Viola bit her lip. Trying to sound casual, she asked, "How is Max, by the way? Did you get him out of the mess he was in?"

"Yes. He's making love to a redhead at the moment. She's witty and sexy and strong and liberated, and he's a little nonplussed because he likes her well enough to think twice about throwing her down and raping her in his usual inimitable style."

Viola laughed. "Maybe I'm a good influence on your writing after all. Maybe Max *is* going to get his consciousness raised."

"No chance," Stephen growled. "I know the ending. He shoots her. He's vaguely sorry, but she's mixed up with the bad guys, and he has to kill her."

"What is she?" she asked sardonically. "The daughter of his lifelong foe?"

"It's either blow her away," said Stephen more slowly, "or declare his love and marry the lady."

"Max isn't capable of love," she said uneasily, doubtful whether they were really talking about Max.

"Max may surprise you," said Stephen.

On Thursday night when he called, Stephen began their conversation by reading her another poem, a piece of light verse deploring, in a series of hilarious rhymes, her refusal to take him to bed. Even as she laughed, she was genuinely impressed by his wittiness.

The conversation wandered vaguely, and Viola sensed that, satirical verse aside, he was not in a laughing mood. He proved this by interrupting something she was telling him about one of her students to say, "Look, love, enough of this chitchat. Tomorrow's Friday, and I want to see you. Conducting a love affair by telephone is not my idea of a fun way to spend a weekend. Leave after school and drive down to the Cape tomorrow. I miss you."

"No. I can't."

"Viola, this week's been hell for me. I'm not getting any writing done, and I have a deadline to meet in a month or so. I'm not sleeping. I want you." His voice was low and intense. "Talking to you like this is torture for me. You sound so close, so warm, so sexy. I feel as if I should be able to reach out and touch you. I keep remembering last Saturday night—the desire in your eyes, the way you moved your lovely body, your cries, your pleasure, your laughter."

"If you don't stop, I'll hang up," she whispered. Her cheeks were flushed, and she felt hot and weak.

"What are you afraid of?" he demanded. "It's good with us; you can't deny it. We've got a special brand of chemistry that's as exhilarating as it is rare. That kind of thing is a gift, Viola. It would be criminal to throw it away."

"You're talking about sex, Stephen. This magical chemistry of yours only refers to the way we relate physically."

"From your tone I infer that you want something more. Are you holding out for marriage, darling?"

His sarcasm made her heart pound with anger. "I'm not holding out for anything! I'm trying to get rid of you, remember? You're the one who's intent on stalking me."

"Liar," he whispered into the phone. "I think you're in love with me. But because of Percy and Douglas and your string of meaningless affairs, you can't open up enough to admit it. Well, I'll force you to admit it, dammit." His voice roughened. "I've tried being sweet and gentle and understanding, but it's not working, is it. You're not used to men who treat you decently. You're used to distant, coldhearted Percy and all his copies. You don't know a good thing when it comes and stares you in the face."

"I don't have to listen to this—"

"No, you don't," he agreed. "I'm not going to waste my time wooing you long-distance any longer, Viola. Why should I, when we both know that the moment I take you in my arms, your objections will turn to water?"

"That might be true," she said, her lips trembling with emotion, "but I feel compelled to remind you that even if you seduce my body, you won't touch my mind, my heart, or my soul!"

"Spoken like a true romantic," he taunted. "It's your body I want, darling. It's your body I intend to have."

It was Saturday morning before she heard from him again. She had passed two restless nights, expecting any minute to find him pounding on her door, but he tantalized her far more by doing nothing. By night she tossed in bed, and when she slept, she had nightmares. By day she fantasized about him, unable to stop her imagination from endlessly picturing her passionate surrender. His tactics were working.

Saturday brought another special-delivery parcel. Ripping it open she discovered a carbon copy of Stephen's rewritten article about Percy. Paper-clipped to the first page was a hand-scrawled note that read, "This is the final draft. I believe it fairly represents the situation. If you have any objections, call me. I intend to send it off next week."

She sat down and read it through, and by the time she reached the final paragraph she was sick with anger. It was even more damaging than it had looked in rough form, written as it was in Stephen's crisp, no-nonsense, faintly sarcastic style. Although the article made no mention of Viola's part in the creation of *An Intricate Solution,* it thoroughly damned her father for stealing a plot, and it even hinted that he may have done that sort of thing all the time. No matter how much revising of her feelings toward her father Viola had done in the past week, there was no way she was going to sit back and allow such a travesty to be published.

She phoned Stephen immediately. When he answered, she launched directly into her tirade. "If you publish this article, I'll sue you for every penny Maxwell Trencher has ever earned you."

"Why? I thought your eyes were finally opened to the subject of honorable, decent old Percy."

"This is a filthy, rotten, despicable thing to do, Stephen! It only proves what I've suspected all along—that all you really care about is some perverted form of petty revenge."

"Revenge isn't petty. Look at *Hamlet,* for instance."

"Don't *Hamlet* me! I've told you my father was ill when he was putting that book together. He must have forgotten that the story was yours. It was an honest mistake, not a case of deliberate plagiarism."

"A writer doesn't forget which stories he's written and which he hasn't," he retorted. "I'm not going to argue with you. The article is finished, and it's going out. I refuse to see *An Intricate Solution* go into one edition after another with Percy continuing to get the credit for it. No writer would sit back and allow that to happen. No literary critic with any integrity would either, Viola, and you know it."

This hurt, for it was true. She couldn't speak, so she hung up instead. Later, when she had cooled off, she called him back.

"I don't want to talk to you until you can restrain your Quentin family indignation," he warned her.

"Stephen, please don't publish your article," she said as humbly as she could manage. "It will destroy my father's reputation."

"You're being melodramatic, Viola."

"Look, I agree that it wouldn't be fair to you for this *mix-up*—she stressed the word—"to be perpetuated. I'm offering you a compromise. Suppress the article, and I'll report the whole story in my biography. I'll interview you and let you have your say, and I promise I won't cover anything up. You'll get the credit you deserve that way; it just won't be so vituperative if it's put in the words of a basically sympathetic biographer. And I promise you the novel will never be reprinted. What do you say?"

"No."

"Stephen, please! Let's talk about it, at least. You owe me that much, dammit."

"Very well," he unexpectedly agreed. "We'll talk about it, but not on the phone. You get into your car and come down here, and we'll discuss it."

"No."

"Yes. I always do business face to face. Take it or leave it, Professor."

"All right, face to face," she conceded slowly. "But not at your place, and not here either. I'll meet you somewhere neutral."

"Somewhere neutral," he repeated with a sardonic lilt. He considered, then said, "Okay, since you're so paranoid about me, I'll meet you where I always meet my agent. We'll have dinner at the Hyatt Regency in Cambridge. Meet me in the lobby. Can you manage that? How's your ankle?"

"Better," she said grimly. "I'll manage it. What time?"

"Seven-thirty."

"I'd rather meet you in that Indian restaurant you told me about, not in some hotel."

"Even in a hotel, darling, I can hardly molest you over cocktails and dinner for two. I'd have to get you into a room first, wouldn't I?"

"Knowing you—" she began.

He cut in, saying, "Look, my coy mistress, you bring your car, I'll bring mine, and the moment we finish dinner you can go home to your lonely bed in Whittacre while I return sorrowfully to the Cape. Does that scenario make you feel secure?"

"No," she retorted. "But I'll be there at seven-thirty anyway. I can't let you do this to my father."

"It's a helluva reason to accept a date," he said wryly. "But I suppose it'll have to do."

Viola pulled into the garage of the Hyatt Regency, the modern, pyramid-shaped hotel on the banks of the Charles River, precisely on time. She took the elevator to the hotel lobby, walking quickly past shops filled with antiques and Chinese imports. The light cape she wore over her black silk cocktail dress with the thin spaghetti straps swirled around her body as she stopped short near the indoor gardens of tall ferns and flowering greenery and looked around for Stephen.

Her eyes slipped right past a tall man in a fashionable dark pin-striped suit as she looked for somebody in blue jeans with a collegiate air about him. She did a double take when the elegant stranger moved smoothly to her side and placed a hand on her bare arm.

"Good evening, Professor," he said, smiling with his lips only. His eyes took in the severe style of her hair, then lowered to sweep insolently over the length of her body in the black sheath. It was a possessive, predatory evaluation, and although it raised her hackles, it also generated an unwelcome heat inside her, which she strove to hide.

"Good evening," she said coolly, returning his stare. He wasn't wearing his glasses, she noticed, and his curly black hair had been cropped into a chic new style. "What on earth happened to you?" she added just before he inclined his head and firmly kissed her lips. He smelled faintly of a musky male cologne, something she had never known him to wear.

She'd never seen him wear a three-piece suit, either, or a white silk shirt, or highly polished Italian leather shoes. He reminded her of someone, she thought with a thread of uneasiness. She couldn't quite think who it was.

"I decided to dress for the occasion," he informed her, taking her arm in a proprietary manner and leading her toward the colorful central atrium of the hotel. Huge potted plants brushed at them, and reflecting pools caught and threw back their image as they walked. Viola felt a little as if she were lost in the jungle. "You're going to learn what it means to be stalked," he had threatened. Great. A jungle atmosphere was just what she needed to put herself at ease.

"It's hardly an occasion that requires formal dress. We're here to discuss business," she reminded him, indicating the manila folder she held against her chest. It contained the revisions in her biography of Percy Quentin, which she had worked on all afternoon—revisions that described the process of creating *An Intricate Solution*.

"Of course," he agreed complacently, swinging his free arm to reveal the hand-tooled black leather briefcase he was carrying.

The sight of it sent a flash of apprehension ripping through her, nearly rooting her to the spot. Above them, angular glassed-in elevators soared into the upper reaches of the hotel, and somewhere a piano player produced a soft ripple of jazz as Viola stared stupidly at Stephen. Who went around in expensive suits and silk shirts, wearing a heavy gold ring like the one Stephen was sporting tonight? Who carried his gun in a black leather briefcase? Maxwell Trencher. She was out for the evening with Maxwell Trencher. And he was looking at her as if he would welcome the idea of shooting her, after the obligatory rape.

He noticed her hesitation, and his hold on her arm tightened. "Still limping, I see. Why aren't you wearing a bandage on that ankle, darling? It's only been a week."

"My ankle is fine, but you're hurting my arm."

His mouth turned up in what she swore was a satisfied smile before he released her, and she abruptly recalled

another of his recent threats: "I'll unleash Max on you."
She shivered.

"Chinese or Continental?" he asked her, consulting
the restaurant directory.

"Continental. I had Chinese last night."

She hoped he'd think she'd had it with a date instead
of alone with her wok and her beef strips and pea pods,
but he didn't rise to that one. He simply pointed the way
up the escalator that led to the second level, where the
Continental restaurant was located.

She could feel his breath on the back of her neck as
he stood just one step behind her on the escalator. His
nearness engendered a soft melting inside her, the warmth
of which astonished her. She reminded herself that such
feelings were her enemy, that she must resist them. He
had been her lover, yes, but that was over.

"I thought you couldn't see without your glasses," she
said as the maître d' led them to a table in the crowded
terrace-style restaurant.

"Contact lenses," he replied. "And I can see well
enough to note that you've defiantly done your hair in
the manner I detest." His eyes moved over her body
again as he helped her remove her cape. "I approve of
your dress, however."

She arched her eyebrows. She was beginning to regret
having worn the black silk. The neckline was too low,
and he seemed fascinated with the place where her simple
gold locket lay against the curve of her breasts.

"What's in the briefcase?" she demanded as he placed
it carefully on one of the extra chairs. "A gun to blow
me away with?"

His lips curled in a smile. "Now why would you think
something like that?"

"You know perfectly well why."

"Do I?" He addressed her with grave, out-of-character
politeness. There was something tight and controlled about
him tonight; his usual air of lightheartedness was miss-
ing. Somehow the cut of his suit made him seem both
taller and broader than she remembered—more power-

ful, more dangerous. Without the trace of humor about his mouth, his expression was formal, cold, and rather ruthless.

"I'd like a drink," she said precipitously.

He nodded to a waiter, who hurriedly approached. "Nervous?" he asked her, ordering martinis for them both.

"Not exactly," she lied. "I would like to know, however, whom I'm having dinner with tonight—Stephen Silkwood or Maxwell Trencher."

"They're the same man," he said calmly.

"You've been telling me all along they were different."

"I've been lying."

She shivered again. "What do you mean, you've been lying? I don't find this amusing, Stephen, your dressing up like Max deliberately to intimidate me. You know I don't like the tough-guy, macho type."

"I don't care what type you like," he said impatiently. "Tonight I intend to please myself."

"What is that supposed to mean?"

He merely smiled.

"You're angry," she said after a pause. She was twisting all the starch out of the linen napkin in her lap. "What do *you* have to be angry about? If anyone has a reason to be upset—"

"Yes, I know; it's you, not me," he interrupted. "You're the one, after all, who's trying to defend poor, dead, misunderstood Percy against the big guns of mean, nasty, wealthy, successful me. All he has is you—pale, lovely, sweet-bodied you—bravely keeping the wolf from the door. It's enough to wrench the heart of the devil himself."

"Oh, come on, Stephen. You don't seriously believe I see it that way." Was he feeling guilty? she wondered.

"How you see it I can't imagine. I'm describing the view from the vantage point of the wolf."

"I don't think that rather tired metaphor is applicable to you and me. That is, you may consider yourself a wolf, but I certainly don't see myself as your prey."

The familiar mischievous light suddenly danced in his green eyes. "Oh, but you are, darling. Tonight especially, that's exactly what you are."

She was spared the necessity of making a reply by the waiter coming back with their drinks.

"A toast," Stephen said, holding out his glass. She raised her own and looked at him expectantly. "To casual weekend affairs."

She clinked her glass defiantly. "May we both enjoy many more of them—with other partners," she added maliciously.

His eyes narrowed. "In the future, certainly. But this weekend you're here, with me."

She took a long swallow of her drink to calm her. The penetrating look in his eyes excited her far more than she cared to admit. "We've agreed to go our separate ways after dinner tonight," she reminded him. "I wouldn't have come otherwise."

"You've made that perfectly clear."

"But you're hoping to change my mind?"

"I never reveal what I'm hoping for this early in the evening," he answered coolly.

She was upset. "I've told you, Stephen, I don't want any further involvement with you. I just can't handle it."

"What about it can't you handle?"

The pain, she thought miserably. The fact that you don't love me. The fact that you can sit there, looking so damnably calm and collected while I tear at my gut to hide the depth of my feelings for you.

"Viola?" he prodded when she didn't speak.

She forcibly hardened herself. "I thought we were going to talk about your article. That's the only reason I came."

His expression darkened. "All right. Talk."

The waiter came for their orders, and while they waited for their food, Viola pulled out her notes from the manila envelope and set about explaining her proposal for placating Stephen. He listened without interruption, reading

without comment the rough material she handed him.
She tried to guess what he thought from his expression,
but his face was difficult to read tonight. His lack of
response made her talk more rapidly from nervousness.

"It ends abruptly because I ripped up the last page I'd
written, which told the world that you held a grudge
against my father because of his affair with your wife.
I'm writing a literary biography, not a history of Daddy's
sex life. Embarrassing matters like adultery can surely,
without dishonesty, be suppressed."

He looked at her, his green gaze searing her soul.
"Percy's dead," he reminded her. "It's me you don't want
to embarrass, isn't it?"

She shrugged noncommittally.

Stephen's fingers played with his silverware. "After
all, I was the fool. Percy made me look like a weak,
credulous cuckold."

"Which is why you still hate him after all these years."

He shook his head. "That may be part of it, but it
wasn't the only reason."

She sighed. "Oh, no. Don't tell me there's some other
dramatic revelation I haven't heard yet."

"You've heard it. I hate him for dragging you into
his plots, for telling me that you tried to seduce me on
that beach to keep me away from his tryst with Carol."

Shakily she said, "I thought you believed me when I
said that wasn't true."

"I do believe you, now. Then, I believed him, and I
blamed him for ruining you, for corrupting his own
daughter and turning her into a fledgling whore at the
age of seventeen. That was his biggest sin as far as I
was concerned. I didn't care all that much about Carol;
our marriage was over anyway. I did care about you,
Viola. You were the main reason I hated him."

She sat there, flushed, listening to these unbelievable
words. It was the closest he'd come to a declaration of
affection, and she wanted to leap to the conclusion that
there was hope, that she needn't be hurt by him after all.
But her brain warned her to be careful, not to get carried

away. He had been looking at her covetously all evening; he wanted her. And he was, as she had already learned, an expert at the art of seduction.

"I thought you loved Carol," she protested, seizing on the one thing she had assumed to be a certainty.

"I thought I did, too, when I married her. But we were too young, only twenty-one, both of us. Within a year or two the marriage was in trouble, and by the time I met you, whatever love I'd had for her had long since died."

She was perplexed. "You didn't love Carol," she said mechanically. "Did you love me?"

He considered. "It might have come to that if your father hadn't screwed it up."

"What about now?" she heard herself say.

"Now you're the one who's screwing it up."

She wasn't sure what to make of that, and before she could decide, their dinner came, fillet of sole amandine for her and New York sirloin for him.

Stephen stared at her for a moment, then said, "Look, I'm bored with all this rehashing of the past, darling. It's pointless; what's done is done. We can't change it. The best we can do is try to understand it, and even that is relatively futile." He paused. "I'll think about your offer with the biography. You're being more than fair; I'll concede that right now. I'll consider everything you've said and let you know what I decide."

She drew a deep breath. "When?"

"Soon." He reached out and covered her hand with his as she reached for her wineglass. His fingers felt warm and reassuring. "Let's talk about something else," he added.

"What else?"

"Darling, we are two reasonably articulate people. I can't believe there aren't a dozen subjects that will spring to life as soon as we touch upon them. Did you read the editorial in the *Globe* today?"

He was right. Within five minutes he had engaged her in an argument about Boston politics, which ranged into a discussion of national politics and global affairs.

At one point he said, "It's great to converse with a woman who's not afraid to disagree with me. I enjoy a good debate almost as much as I like a warm tussle in bed."

She shifted uncomfortably, dynamically aware of the magnetic pull between them. There was a sexual undercurrent to their spirited arguing, and it was subtly magnified tonight by Stephen's uncanny resemblance to Maxwell Trencher. He wouldn't have dressed like this, she reasoned, unless he had some plan in mind. He probably had every intention of forcing her into his car and dragging her off to the Cape.

As she nervously gulped her coffee, Viola glanced surreptitiously at her watch. It was only nine-thirty, and they were finished with dinner. It was early, and she was enjoying his company, but she was going to have to make some move to leave. She would have to be firm, to ignore the warmth in his eyes, to forget that underneath that dignified suit was a muscular male body that had once merged ecstatically with her own. They had agreed to separate after dinner. If she gave even an inch on that agreement, she knew they would end up together either at his place or hers, and all her efforts to disentangle herself from this dead-end relationship would have been wasted.

Still, she couldn't bring herself to object when he suggested that they go to the cocktail lounge on the top floor of the building for an after-dinner drink.

"It revolves like a carousel," he told her. "There's a spectacular view of Boston."

"One drink, then," she agreed as he took her arm and led her to the elevators. He was still holding the black briefcase, which he hadn't opened during dinner. She wondered again, a little uneasily, what was in it.

In the elevator he stood opposite her, his eyes studying hers, and she remembered with dramatic intensity the elevator on the Whittacre campus where they'd been trapped. The memory of it made her ache with desire.

Such behavior would be impossible here. The elevator was a glass cage, open to the interior atrium of the hotel. As it rose smoothly over the terrace where they had eaten their dinner, Viola stared down into the shining fountains and lush plants in the lobby below, thankful for the excuse to avoid his gaze. She had never felt so edgy with him before.

Stephen took her arm again as the elevator stopped, leading her firmly out into the hotel corridor. They passed a series of cream-colored doors with numbers on them— 1403, 1404, 1405.

"Are we on the right floor?" she asked him. "I thought the cocktail lounge was on fifteen."

Stephen—or was it Max—looked at her wordlessly and smiled. They rounded a corner, and he stopped outside 1407. Putting down his briefcase, he fitted a key into the lock, keeping firm hold of her with his other hand.

"Inside, darling," he said menacingly, giving her a gentle shove as the door swung open. She found herself in a tastefully decorated hotel room, staring in dismay at a king-sized bed. Stephen tossed his briefcase onto a chair and turned to lock the door.

She whirled to face him, feeling like a total idiot. "What the hell do you think you're doing?" she cried, moving back toward the door.

He blocked her way with his body, standing between her and escape, tall and strong and as ruthless as Maxwell Trencher. "I called from the Cape and reserved a room," he announced calmly. "I checked in before meeting you downstairs. I never had the slightest intention of allowing you to leave tonight."

She felt the heat from her anger staining her face and neck crimson. "Unfortunately for you, this is a public hotel. I'm certain they don't take kindly to their male guests waylaying unwilling women on the way to the cocktail lounge. If you touch me, I'll scream the place down."

"I wouldn't advise that," he whispered, folding his

arms around her and bending his face to hers. "You don't really want the hotel management involved in our private struggles, do you?" His mouth moved sensuously over hers, cutting off her disclaimer. He kissed her long and deeply, pressing her against his body until she could feel his heat despite the barrier of their clothes. "Accept it, darling," he crooned. "Tonight is the night I'm calling all your bluffs."

His tongue darted out and skimmed over the surface of her lips, causing exquisite shivers of delicate pleasure to run through her. She felt herself caving in. Desperately she clenched her fists against his chest and tried to push him away.

"No, Stephen, I don't want this. Please let me go."

"Impossible," he breathed, running hot hands over her bare shoulders and up her neck to her hair. He began unknotting it. She struggled, trying to step on his toes and kick him at the same time. He responded by pinning one of her arms behind her in a firm grip that brought tears of rage and frustration to her eyes.

"Stephen!" she cried.

"Max," he corrected. "Tonight you're in the clutches of Max Trencher, darling, who won't think twice about using force to get what he wants."

"I don't think that's funny!"

"It's not meant to be funny, Professor. It's meant to frighten you out of your wits," he said lightly. His slight smile seemed to belie his words. Swinging her up into his arms, he carried her across the room to the bed.

# CHAPTER
## *Eleven*

STEPHEN SET VIOLA down on her feet beside the mammoth hotel bed, which was primly covered by a linen counterpane. He kept one arm firmly around her waist, and his green eyes glittered as he stared down into hers.

"I want you to undress," he said in a low voice. "You know how I like it—nice and slow and sensual."

"Go to hell," she snapped.

"I'm asking you politely. Refuse me, and I'll get nasty."

Aware of his hard, tense body towering over her, Viola felt the first thrill of fear. "If I act masterful, it's to excite us both," he had told her last weekend, but she was by no means sure that he was acting now. Where did Stephen end and Max begin? Had she finally pushed him over the line? In some dark way, Stephen Silkwood was still a mystery to her. Was he the lively, imaginative, aggressive-yet-civilized lover he'd appeared to be last weekend? Or was he basically a brute, like Max?

"I don't believe this." She was trying to keep her voice steady. "If this is a game, I don't want to play."

"Strip," was his reply.

"Damn you! I won't take my clothes off on the orders of any man!"

His eyebrows arched, and his hold on her shifted. She tensed as he sought the zipper at the back of her dress and jerked it downward. It caught. Undaunted, he slipped the spaghetti straps off her shoulders and pushed at the still-tight material covering her breasts. Viola tried to shove him away, but his fingers snagged in the fragile silk. There was an oddly sensual sound as the bodice ripped.

Stephen grinned as he treated her exposed, braless breasts to a stare that seemed to lick them with fire. "How nice," he drawled. "I've always wanted to do that to some recalcitrant female. Max gets to have all the fun."

His hot fingers immediately captured the softness of her, but her blood was beating so hard in her ears that she was only half-conscious of his light, provocative touch. With her dress destroyed, she could hardly run out into the hallway. She was trapped.

"How dare you?" she choked, trembling with a bewildering combination of anger and incipient arousal. "This was an expensive dress, damn you!"

"I'll buy you another," he whispered, caressing the fullness of her breasts with his fingertips, then bending his head to suck deliciously on one hardening nipple. "You're beautiful, sweetheart," he added more tenderly.

His gentle hands on her body and the familiar warmth of his breath calmed her anxiety. The wine she had drunk with dinner, combined with the crisp, masculine scent of him, the large bed just behind her, and the sparkling lights of the city shining through the huge windows opposite their entwined forms all conspired to weaken her resistance.

She ached to respond to his lovemaking, even if it

meant submitting to his domination. Hunger uncoiled in her loins, and before she could stop herself the fingers of one of her hands had found their way into his sleek, dark hair. Oh, Lord, she wanted him! All week she had longed for this. How could she continue to fight?

"Stephen," she breathed, as his tongue flicked over the nub of one breast in a rapid, snakelike motion. "Why do I let you do this to me?"

He flashed her a confident grin as he worked the silk material of her ruined dress down over her hips to expose the rest of her body. "Because you love me?" he suggested.

She stiffened. "I don't love you!"

The grin faded, and his hands were less gentle as he disposed of both the dress and the half-slip she wore beneath it. "Excuse me. Of course you don't," he said harshly. "I forgot. You're a Quentin. The members of your family don't allow themselves to love anybody. Lust, however, is a different story. When it comes to lust and casual affairs, the Quentins aren't so squeamish."

He pushed her back to arm's length to stare at the brief triangle of her bikini panties, which was all that covered her now. He favored her with a construction-site whistle. "You look fantastic, Professor. I am thoroughly seduced."

Despite the intimacy they'd shared the previous weekend, Viola was embarrassed by his frankly appreciative stare, which lingered on her breasts and thighs with all the heat of a touch. It didn't help matters that he was still completely dressed in his dignified, three-piece suit. She sat down suddenly on the edge of the bed.

"I could kill you for doing this to me," she seethed.

"It's okay," he murmured against her lips as he bent to kiss her. He stood over her, his legs straddling her bare thighs, and she was acutely conscious of the leashed power in his strong, lanky body. "Just relax, darling, and trust me."

*Trust me.* So it *was* a game. One of his dominant-male sexual fantasies, no doubt. She was supposed to play along and enjoy being Maxwell Trencher's latest victim.

"Your arrogance deserves a trophy," she muttered, silently assessing the merits of surprising him with a well-aimed blow to the groin. Her knees were pinned, but her hands were free, and he was positioned about right for it. But what if she injured him? she thought ridiculously.

"Forget it!" he said so sharply that her nerves shimmered and jumped. Could he read her mind? she wondered as she had several times before. "I'm not going to hurt you," he added very softly. "Relax."

He lifted his mouth just off hers and ran his tongue over her lips with the bewitching delicacy she couldn't resist. She could feel the heat gathering in the pit of her stomach, surging upward to leap through her veins like wildfire. He gently swept the pins from her hair until it fell in a cloud around her face.

"Why not just accept it?" he asked against her cheekbones, his lips moving lightly to taste every tiny freckle on her pale skin. "Your feelings for me are stronger than you admit." His tongue moved to her ear and probed it sensuously, creating little waves that reverberated deep in the secret core of her. His fingers circled a breast, glided over the bareness of her waist, and molded a hipbone while his teeth delivered a playful nip to her ear.

She moaned faintly, her head falling forward to rest against his muscled chest beneath the well-tailored suit jacket. She could feel his heart beating in rapid thuds against her cheek. Slowly, unable to stop herself, she reached for the buttons of his vest.

"That's right, sweetheart," he said in the same cocky voice he'd been employing off and on ever since he'd brought her into the room. His hand slipped down into her panties to invade the traitorous warmth between her legs. "You're moist for me, aching for me. You're the last woman on earth I'd ever have to force."

And that, damn him, was too much. She tried to push him away. "Don't be so sure, Stephen," she retorted furiously. "Stop assaulting me!"

"I've hardly even begun," he said, pushing her back on the bed and wrestling the bedclothes out from under her so she lay in the coolness of the sheets. She sat up like a shot as soon as he released her to rip at his own buttons, but she resisted the wild idea of dashing for the door. She was naked, for heaven's sake.

Circling her knees with her arms, she watched him undress. It was dark—only one light was switched on on the dressing table at the far side of the spacious room— and as he stripped off his elegant suit and shirt in the dusky light, Stephen looked like a lustful stranger. His powerful desire for her was intoxicating; she was forced to admit that. And she didn't seriously believe he would hurt her.

He tossed his clothes to the floor with a carelessness that sent an unexpected flash of amusement rippling through her. He wouldn't look so smooth and dignified in the morning. "Max always hangs up his clothes," she said. "He's a brute, but an extremely neat and orderly one."

He came toward her, naked and magnificent as always. His lean, hard body, long-limbed and smooth of muscle, the black mat of hair spreading wide over his chest, then narrowing to a thin band over his stomach and down . . . the proud thrust of his manhood afire for her. How could she resist him?

"Yeah?" he whispered, his smoldering eyes locking with hers. "Are you suggesting that my mask is slipping? Well, so is yours, lady. The timid-virgin act went over well eleven years ago, but no longer, darling."

He let himself down on the bed beside her and ran the pad of one finger over the surface of her left breast. He circled the nipple slowly, watching the tip harden in anticipation of his touch. Viola sucked in her breath but didn't stir. His other hand closed on her scalp and held her steady for his kiss. "Fight me some more," he muttered enticingly against her lips. "I want to ravish you tonight."

She was getting pulled into the fantasy in spite of herself. Her breasts were tingling; her lower body felt heavy and awash with need. She wanted him. "Trust me," he had whispered, and she was beginning to. It was only a game, a game she could relax and enjoy. There was nothing to be afraid of.

"You okay?" His voice was a breath against her ear.

She nodded, her hair brushing his face. He groaned with pleasure as he tugged on her earlobe with his teeth. Then his legs tangled with hers as he slowly moved to press her down beneath him. Slipping more completely into the fantasy, she pushed against his shoulders and turned her head away from his kiss. For several seconds the strength in her arms held him off while he concentrated on stilling her head with one commanding hand in her hair. He found her mouth and invaded, pushing past her teeth with his tongue, increasing her arousal with every lick and nip and brush of his mouth. Then his hands clamped on her slender wrists, and he pinned her.

"Gotcha!" he whispered, easily restraining her. A muscled thigh pressed intimately between her legs while his hips covered hers with a pressure that made his desire all too obvious.

If she hadn't still been wearing her panties, Viola suspected that he would have ended their struggle by taking her immediately. As it was, he held her motionless and teased her with his skillful fingers and maddening tongue, whispering erotic threats in her ears. In spite of her spiraling excitement, Viola felt a slight twinge of anxiety as it occurred to her that he seemed to be thoroughly enjoying her subjugation.

She'd better stop fighting, he warned her finally, or he'd have to unpack the contents of his black leather briefcase. Viola had a sudden, unnerving image of Max.

"I'm your master, sweetheart," Stephen added, oblivious to her abrupt stiffening. "From now on, always and forever, you'll surrender to me or you'll pay the price."

As the low, sexy words threaded themselves into her brain, Viola felt a cramp inside her, physical at first, but turning swiftly into something deeper, darker, stronger. She began to tremble as panic grabbed her, dragging her down and smothering her desire in a bottomless well of fear.

"You bitch!" Douglas had screamed at her on their last terrible night together. "You've pushed me too far this time, and now you're going to pay the price."

Then she was huddled in a corner of the women's shelter, her nose bleeding, her eyes darkening to blackness, her entire body shaking with terror and pain. Around her were the haunted, blank-eyed faces of the other women, some of them clutching silent, traumatized children. They were victims, the sort of people Viola was used to seeing occasionally on the nightly news—the poor, hapless women to whose charitable cause she had now and then sent a check in an attempt to save them from their misery. I don't look like that, Viola had told herself, averting her eyes when a young woman with bruises all over her face had offered her a tentative smile. I would never allow some man to do that to me. I'm not one of them. I'm not, I'm not. I can't be one of them!

She didn't realize she had spoken aloud until she heard Stephen's concerned voice saying, "One of whom, darling? You're not one of whom?"

He had shifted his weight off her and was holding her undemandingly against his side, warming her chilled, shivering body with his arms and kissing away the tears that were cascading down her cheeks. "Easy, sweetheart," he whispered over and over. "Easy."

She pressed her head into his shoulder and managed a strangled laugh. "You got your wish," she said. "I'm frightened out of my wits."

He said only one word, but it proved that he understood. "Douglas?"

Her whimpers escalated to full-fledged sobs.

He did not try to stop the flow of her tears, but held

her closely, gently massaging her shaking limbs and murmuring soothing words in her ear. What he had done with his sexual frustration she couldn't imagine, but as the worst of the convulsive weeping began to let up, she half wished that he wouldn't be so controlled and understanding. It only made her feel worse. He'd started out the evening behaving like a macho, aggressive brute. Why did he have to switch back to being the tender, affectionate lover whose arms she never wanted to leave? It would be so much easier to hate him if he were really Max.

When at last the shuddering sobs stopped, Viola was exhausted, but, disconcertingly, the pain was still there, gnawing at her insides. Her nerves felt raw and exposed, as if her skin were stripped off, opening the very core of her to the light and the air. He'd done it, she realized sickly as this image struck her. He had torn down her defenses and reached the inner self, the last part of her, which she had so desperately tried to keep from him. She was open to him now, defenseless.

She let out a little moan at this conclusion, and again he said, rubbing his thumbs gently over her cheekbones, "One of whom, Viola? What did you mean when you cried out that you weren't one of them?"

"The women . . . in the shelter," she said unwillingly. "They had battered faces and blank, staring eyes. I didn't want to admit that I looked just like them . . . but of course I did."

She paused, shivering. Being defenseless meant she couldn't even lie to herself anymore, let alone to him. "I couldn't face up to the fact that, like them, I had lived with and loved a man who was capable of doing that to me."

She raised her eyes to his briefly, then dropped them again. He had propped himself up on his elbow beside her, and his fingers were stroking the tear-dampened hair back from her face. "Obviously there's something in me that's perversely attracted to brutal, domineering men."

His expression darkened. "Meaning me?"

"I must be masochistic," she went on recklessly. "I always fall in love with men who want little more than to hurt me."

"Don't put me in the same category with Douglas, Viola," he said warningly, the patience gone from his voice. "I'm not violent, and I would never deliberately hurt you."

"No?" she cried, anger flaming in her with swift, passionate intensity. "What do you call this, then, Stephen? Do I look and sound like the picture of serene mental health? A few minutes ago I went along with your horrid little game. I was even excited by it! I let you talk me into meeting you tonight, and I let you trick me into this hotel room and rip off my dress even though I knew— I *knew* Stephen—that you were just doing it out of ... of lust! I'm talking about emotional pain, Stephen. You deal it out, and I open my arms and take it!"

Before she had finished, he had rolled off the bed and stalked over to the window, where he stood, tall and naked and so beautiful in her eyes that she could have screamed with the pain of not possessing him. He pressed his hands against the glass, looking as hard and tense as a statue. He was breathing in rasps. Beyond him the lights of Boston glowed like stars over the darkly flowing water of the Charles River.

Trembling, Viola sat up in bed, clutching her knees. "This is ridiculous," she said starkly. "What are you doing?"

He turned so suddenly that she jumped, and he frowned at this evidence of her nervousness. "Easy," he repeated, in a tone that was anything but. "If I have to keep away from you to convince you that I'm not going to hurt you, then that's what I'll do."

"It's too late. The damage is done."

"Dammit, Viola, I didn't really mean to frighten you. It was a calculated risk. You'd told me about Douglas and what he'd done to you. And I knew you didn't trust me. But I had to break through to you somehow." His voice was low but pregnant with feeling. "I had to find some way to tear down that wall. What the hell was I supposed to do? All week I've bent over backwards trying to be the caring, witty, considerate lover, but nothing seemed to move you. Max Trencher was my last card in this bitter little game between us. If *he* couldn't get through to you, nobody could."

"What are you talking about?" she demanded, confused and disturbed by his defeated tone. He sounded as if he were in just as much pain as she was. He even looked as if he might cry, too.

"Last weekend you were warm and open and joyous in my arms," he went on, pacing back over the thick-piled carpet toward her. "I don't understand what happened to change you. I thought, after finding you again, that this time, finally, everything would work for us. But it's not working, and it's your fault." He had reached her; one of his hands stretched out to grip her shoulder. Her red hair flowed over his hand as if the two belonged together.

"You're a coward, Viola," he went on, no longer troubling to hide the despair in his voice. "You're beautiful and brilliant and strong. You've got everything I've ever looked for in a woman except one thing: you're afraid to love, dammit. You're afraid to take the risk."

She tossed her head back to meet the intense glare of his sea-green eyes, her heart alight with sudden hope. "And you, Stephen? Are you afraid to love?" she whispered.

"Arrogant I may be. Aggressive I certainly am. But afraid I'm not. I love you. Dear God, isn't it obvious?"

His two hands were holding her head now, framing her face while the green flame in his eyes caressed her lips, her hair, her brow with a tenderness that spoke of much more than simple desire. *"Dear God, isn't it obvious?"* Dear God, she had been a fool.

Would lust drive a man to call a woman every day, to listen to her problems and tell her his own, to talk for hours about every subject under the sun? Would the desire for revenge against her father inspire him to send her flowers and write her sonnets, and to accept, until tonight, her irrational demand that they should not meet? Would a desire to hurt her enable him to control his sexual excitement at its peak in order to nestle her close and comfort her?

"Stephen?" she whispered, her fingertips reaching out to touch his lips, then his cheeks and his eyelids and his throat. She could feel his pain, his anger, and his sudden hope as strongly as if they were her own emotions. He would not be looking at her like this, she knew, if what he had spoken had not been true.

"I know it can't be easy for you, sweetheart," he said more gently, "after Percy, after Douglas. They were coldhearted bastards, both of them, and God only knows what damage they've done to you. I know it's difficult for you to trust me, but together we have everything we need. Can't you see that? How can you deny that we were meant for each other?"

"Stephen," she cried, finally finding her tongue, "I had no idea you felt this way! Why didn't you tell me?"

"I'm telling you now."

Viola slid her hands down to hold his upper arms and pulled herself up to a kneeling position against his body as he stood beside the bed. She pressed her head against his chest, where his heart was beating heavily. She kissed his warm, furred chest, inhaling his scent and tasting the saltiness of his skin. "You're right," she said, her voice muffled by the hair that her breath was stirring. "I've been a coward, but that's over, Stephen. I'm not afraid anymore. I was only afraid because I knew how terribly much I loved you, and how hurt I would be when you dumped me."

His arms slipped around her shoulders, his hands under her hair. "So you decided to dump me first?"

Her head came up to meet his eyes as she heard the first returning note of the lightheartedness that had characterized their interaction from the start. There was warmth in his look—and relief. She shot him a smile. "I didn't succeed very well, did I? When it comes to sheer persistence, you take the prize."

"I'm undumpable," he agreed, caressing the nape of her neck in a manner that reminded her they were naked together, or nearly so, and locked in a luxurious hotel room.

Yanking hard on his arms, she pulled him down beside her. He loved her. Nothing mattered but that. Together they would have everything they would ever need. "If you still want to ravish me, Max," she whispered seductively, "I'm ready to comply."

"Ummm," he said as her tongue slipped against his, up and down, in and out, until they both moaned and moved convulsively into a tight, body-to-body embrace.

"Aren't you going to give me the third degree—how long have I loved you, how long will I continue to love you, when's the wedding, all that?" he demanded a little breathlessly.

"Later," she murmured. She *did* trust him, she realized joyfully.

"Does this mean you've decided to play?" he teased. Her hands were all over him now, caressing him as intimately as he had caressed her, enjoying the curly roughness of his body hair, the heated warmth of his muscles.

"Go to the head of the class."

"All right, Professor, but don't get cocky. I'm your master tonight, and you'd better remember it." He pinned her arms to the mattress on either side of her head and kissed her open mouth, drawing her tongue into play with his. His legs proceeded to nudge hers apart. "I don't want to hear any more of this casual-weekend-fling nonsense. From now on I want you on my terms."

"Which are?"

"Sex on demand, for one thing. I'm not going to resort to violence every night; it's too strenuous! In the future, when I order you to strip, I expect instant compliance."

She smiled wickedly. "Yes, master."

"And I expect faithfulness," he said more seriously.

"Get rid of David Newstead and anyone else who may be in the habit of cozying up to you."

"That's easy. David is simply a friend, and, as for the others, they exist only in your nasty imagination. There's only you, Stephen. No one else."

"No casual affairs?"

She shook her head. "You're about as casual as I get."

"I thought as much," he admitted as his hands lovingly teased her breasts. "There was nothing practiced about the way you gave yourself to me last weekend."

"I'm glad you noticed," she whispered. "You're my only love, Stephen. Always and forever," she added, repeating his earlier words.

He sighed and quickened the pace, kissing her more deeply and sliding a hand between their eager bodies to trace a burning path from her breasts to the softness of her belly . . . and lower. She made a sound of pleasure and arched toward his expertly probing fingers. "It feels so good," she moaned, clinging to his shoulders as if he were the only stable thing in her world of rapidly spiraling sensation.

Quite suddenly he lifted himself up to kneel astride her and explore her all over with fiery, tantalizing caresses. Her eyes feasted on him while her body twisted and writhed. His handsome features were darkened by passion; his long, smooth body feathered by dusky curls of hair loomed possessively just above her; his voice was husky and deep as he urged her on to greater pleasure and increasingly uninhibited response. His words became blatantly sexual as his skillful fingers sketched ever smaller and more focused concentric circles around the secret core of her, which was still covered by the wispy material of her panties.

She cried out. Within moments he had her moving rhythmically and breathing in gasps as the enticing assault of his hands was joined by the dazzling play of his tongue against the swells and valleys of her breasts. When she begged for his complete possession, his caresses suddenly roughened. He stripped off her panties with an impatient jerk, then slid lower on the bed so his mouth could take her. Beneath his hot touch, an excited fluttering began, and her entire body tensed in readiness as he swept her up, up, and nearly over the top. He lifted his head, and she groaned in protest, begging him to finish what he'd started.

"I will," he promised with a touch of mischief. "But on my terms, as I told you before."

He moved up and hovered over her quivering body, letting her feel him against her but still not giving her what she needed. "Tell me again that you love me," he demanded. "Convince me. I want everything from you, everything there is of you to give."

Her dazed eyes met and locked with his. "I love you, Stephen," she said in a firm, clear voice. "I love you and trust you with all my heart and soul and mind and blood and muscle. I've loved you ever since I was seventeen years old."

His eyes glowed very green. She could feel him trembling against her as the strain of waiting finally proved too much. Abruptly he moved, entering her with an impact that jolted them both. His rhythms were ragged; neither of them had an ounce of control left. "My sweet Viola," he gasped with his last articulate breath. "My sexy lady."

Their bodies moved together in the ageless, frenzied dance of passion, head to head, heart to heart, legs entwined, and flesh so tightly merged that it was almost impossible to tell where his body ended and hers began. She was so near the edge that the golden melting began almost as soon as he entered her, and it seemed to go on forever, the pleasure-explosions lengthening and deepening until her entire soul felt as if it were pulsing with delight.

After a few seconds of furious striving, he, too, found perfect fulfillment, his heart beating wildly against her breast, his lips soundlessly forming the syllables of her name. A rush of tenderness flooded her as she folded him in her closest embrace, her legs wrapped tightly around his thighs, her hands moving gently over his sweat-slicked shoulders. "I love you," she murmured again. "I love you, Stephen, Max, whoever."

She felt a new convulsion against her and realized he was laughing. He raised his head and grinned down at her. His suave new haircut had turned into a damp, tangled mess. "Whoever?" he repeated, still laughing.

She knocked on his forehead lightly with one fist. "I sometimes think there's a whole cast of characters in there." She paused, smirking. "Who says I'm the only one who laughs at the moment of supreme ecstasy?"

"I'm a changed man, I'll admit it."

They lay quietly for several minutes while their breathing returned to normal. Stephen's hands fondled her absently as she nestled along his side, one of her legs thrown possessively over his thigh.

"Stephen?"

"Yes, my dearest lady?"

"What do you really have in that briefcase of yours?"

Once again she heard his low laugh. "Do you dare to ask me, wench? Whips and cuffs and harnesses and I-don't-know-what-all, designed, my love, to keep you in line."

"Oh, yeah, Max? Show me," she challenged.

He sat up and reached for the briefcase on the chair beside the bed. "Here it is, Pandora. You'll be sorry. Once you open the box, you're at the mercy of everything in it. I will be absolutely ruthless, I promise you. I'll make the Marquis de Sade look like Prince Charming."

She unsnapped the clasps. "What's to stop me from using the stuff on you?" she retorted. "You and your macho-male act. You just wait till you see my slave-mistress routine, you miserable cur."

"Heavens," Stephen breathed, quirking an eyebrow at her. "I'm trembling with anticipation. What time does it start?"

"Whenever I feel like it, and you'd better be ready to

jump to my commands." Opening the briefcase she began to laugh. "Shaving cream? A toothbrush? Papers? Your glasses? Fresh underwear? Very terrifying, Stephen Silkwood! This is your overnight bag."

"Two toothbrushes," he corrected. "Since you, as usual, are traveling without a suitcase." He pushed her down beneath him once again. "Don't knock it," he said lecherously. "You'd be surprised at the terrifying things I can do to you with a toothbrush."

"I'm trembling with anticipation," she parroted. "Show me."

He rolled off her. "What do you expect—miracles? I'm pushing forty, darling. I'll show you later. You should have taken me eleven years ago; you don't know what you missed."

Ignoring his protests, she began kissing and caressing him intimately, and in a little while he pulled her down on top of him saying, "A miracle. I might have known it, witch. I love you."

"You'd better, Max. This is one woman who has no intention of getting blown away in the end."

"No," he said thickly, drawing her down into their exquisite union again. "This time it looks as if old Max has finally met his match."

When she awoke in the morning, Viola rolled over in the big bed but found no warm, cozy body lying next to hers. She opened her eyes and sat up.

"Good morning, sleepyhead," said Stephen from the chair beside the bed. He had his briefcase open on the bedside table and a yellow legal pad in his lap. He was tapping his front teeth with the tip of a pen. "Sleep well?"

"Wonderfully. How long have you been up?"

"Half an hour or so. I was going to run downstairs and buy you some clothes from one of the hotel shops, but I didn't dare leave you alone again, after last weekend."

She clasped her arms around her knees and gazed at him impishly. "I'm not going to take off," she said.

"You're not getting rid of me that easily. What are you writing?"

"Just some ideas for the last couple of chapters of my novel. It's turning out differently than I'd planned."

"May I see?"

"No way. You think I deliberately turn my work over to hostile reviewers?"

"I promise I'll go easy on you this time."

"Ha. That's what they all say."

She slid over next to the chair and tried to look over his shoulder. "Come on, Stephen, let me see. Is Max in bed with the redhead?"

"No," he said, dumping the pad back into the briefcase, "but I'm going to be." He grabbed her and administered a long, sensuous kiss, pulling her into his lap in the process. She nestled against his bare chest and ran her fingers through the thick hair there. He was naked except for his shorts.

"Umm," he whispered. "On second thought, I'm not going to buy you any new clothes. I like you better this way." He stroked her breasts lovingly. "My moon goddess."

"May I point out that the sun is shining brightly out there and it's probably ten o'clock in the morning?"

"No matter. You'll always be a moon goddess to me."

He tried to kiss her again, but she was busy raiding the contents of his briefcase. "No, seriously, I want to see what you're writing. Hey, what's this?"

Under the legal pad at the bottom of the case she found a carbon copy of a typed letter, dated Friday. The address of the periodical to which Stephen had threatened to sell his article about her father leaped out at her. She shot him a wary glance.

He raised his eyebrows. "Snooping again, darling? Go on, read it."

The letter was short and to the point. Stephen thanked the editors for considering his proposal, but on further thought, he had decided that he must have been mistaken in his suspicions. There was no story in it after all, and he was withdrawing the idea.

Viola raised her startled eyes to his. "But this was written before you saw me and heard my offer about the biography."

There was a glint of mischief in his eyes. "True," he acknowledged. "When we met last night, I'd already sent this letter."

"You mean you let me go through all that anguish last night for no reason?" she cried on a rising note of anger. "You made me bargain and grovel and beg!"

"Hey, take it easy. I thought you'd be pleased to find me backing down."

"I am pleased!" she said furiously, sounding so displeased that he broke into laughter, which only made her angrier. "You deliberately manipulated me, Stephen! I wouldn't have come here last night if I'd known I didn't have to talk you out of publishing the blasted article."

"Sorry you came?" he asked softly, fondling one of her nipples with tormenting tenderness.

"You tricked me," she said a little less stridently. "And I fell for it." She shook her head sadly.

"I would have told you at dinner, but I didn't want you to think I expected you to sleep with me as a reward for not publishing. In short, I didn't want Percy's ghost present for our lovemaking."

"So you preferred to resort to force?"

His lips brushed the side of her throat. "Whatever works," he said huskily.

She pulled her head free to ask, "But Stephen, why did you make this decision? It *was* your story. You have a right to clear the matter up." She touched her fingers to his lips. "I love you. Whatever you do with that article, it's not going to make any difference in the way I feel about you." She hesitated a moment, then added, "As you have pointed out numerous times, my father's dead and you're alive. For your sake I want the truth to come out, Stephen."

His eyes considered her seriously. "You really mean that?"

She examined her heart and concluded that she did. Despite everything she had learned about her father, she loved Percy Quentin, and she always would. But she saw him more realistically now; he had been a human being, with imperfections and faults, just like anybody else. He wasn't a saint whose shrine she had to protect at all costs. And as far as his literary reputation was concerned, she could not control its course. His strengths as a writer would shine through in spite of the mistakes he had made at the end of his career. He didn't need her. But Stephen did.

She smiled at him, her love radiating from her earnest eyes. "I mean it. From now on it's your reputation I'm going to defend against would-be detractors. I hereby banish Percy's ghost."

"Come to bed," he said, "and I'll tell you a story of which I am ashamed."

Naked once more together under the sheets, they coiled their bodies together while Stephen spoke. "I told you when you first discovered the roughed-out version of my article that I doubted I would ever publish it. I didn't tell you why. It wasn't only that I was concerned about your negative reaction, although that entered into it, of course. I was more concerned about whether my accusation was really justified."

"What do you mean? You showed me your story. The plot of *An Intricate Solution* was obviously lifted from it."

"Yes, but the fact is, the seminal idea for the story was your father's. I was his student at the time, remember. He suggested I write a mystery based on the twist that a suicide could be staged to resemble a murder. Although I thought it through and developed the characters, the motivation, and the incidents of the plot, the intricate solution, you see, was essentially Percy's."

Viola was confused. "Then why have you been making such a federal case out of it?" she demanded.

"You can't copyright an idea, darling, and the germ of an idea was all it was. I was the one who shaped it into a story, and your father had no right to use that story as the basis for a novel. It infuriated me that he did, but my anger seems to have dissipated. I needed to write the article, I think, to work off my resentment and my pain. That's what I always do with my aggression—channel it into my writing."

"Which is why Max is so violent?"

"You got it. If Max didn't exist, then you might have something to worry about."

"I'm not so sure about that," she said skeptically. "I think you ought to have been born into an earlier century when you could work off your tensions more efficiently in the perennial wars."

"Speaking of working off tensions..."

"Oh, no," she objected as his hands moved provocatively over her. "I still don't entirely understand about your article. Do you intend to hold me to my offer about explaining the matter in my biography?"

"No, I'd rather just let the matter drop."

"But then you don't get credit for everything that's yours in *An Intricate Solution*."

"Neither do you," he pointed out. "Let's just regard it as a family endeavor. Percy provided the basic premise, I provided the plot and the characters, he fleshed it out into a novel, and you polished up the final product."

"Stephen, are you sure?"

"I'm positive," he assured her, kissing her tenderly. "Let's put it behind us." He ran his hands over her bare shoulders and down along her spine to the small of her back. She shivered and pressed against his muscled flesh while he smoothed her breasts and dropped soft kisses from her hairline to the hollow above her collarbone. "I can't get enough of you," he murmured ardently. "My desire for you is like a fever: I take a cure every couple of hours, but my temperature keeps shooting right back up again."

She reveled in the feeling of his hard, flat stomach

pressed to hers, the possessive repositioning of his legs astride hers. "A little physical therapy might help," she whispered.

"What a coincidence. I was just thinking the same thing."

"I love you, Stephen," she told him as his exquisite courting of her body began all over again. "Forever. I'll always love you."

"I'm going to hold you to that, Professor."

# CHAPTER
## *Twelve*

"COLERIDGE DESCRIBES IAGO as a creature of motiveless malignancy," Viola was telling her large lecture class in Shakespearean tragedy on a Friday afternoon several weeks later. It was just about the end of the year, and her students were crowded in to hear her final words of wisdom before their exam. Some of them had boyfriends with them, Viola noticed, seeing several male faces in the lecture hall. That frequently happened on a Friday afternoon. "Although Iago has several ostensible reasons for his hatred toward Othello, none of them seems sufficient to justify his extreme villainy."

A hand went up at the back of the hall, but it was dark there, and she couldn't make out the student's face. "Does someone have a question back there?" she asked.

"Yes," said a jaunty male voice. Viola flushed with pleasure at the familiar sound. It was Stephen. She hadn't seen him for ten days because he had been so hard at work on his novel. "Don't you think Coleridge was exaggerating? If I remember correctly, Iago accuses Othello of having cuckolded him. When someone has slept with your wife, it seems reasonable that the injured party should seek revenge, don't you think, Professor?"

"You raise the moral question of whether revenge is ever justifiable," she returned, smiling.

"I doubt that Iago was interested in moral questions. He simply sought to avenge himself in the most direct manner, by corrupting the wife of the man who had allegedly injured him. What's so remarkable about that? It's quite a modern mentality, I would say. I'll bet it happens all the time."

Several of the young women in the lecture hall giggled and turned to look at this troublemaker.

"You think so?" Viola said easily. "You find the play credible, then? Excellent, because its credibility, of course, has always been one of the main objections to *Othello*, ever since Thomas Rymer described it in 1693 as so much ado about a handkerchief."

Stephen took the hint and kept his mouth shut while she went on with her lecture.

After class, George Denton stopped Viola outside the hall. "An excellent lecture, my dear," he told her. "I sat in for a while. I intend to put a very complimentary review of your teaching abilities in your dossier. It should help you when it comes time for you to be considered for tenure."

Viola was both pleased and flustered; she hadn't realized her department chairman was sitting in. She was grateful she hadn't been able to see him; she would have been nervous as hell. "Thank you, George," she said.

"I thought you handled that disruptive student, or whoever he was, very well," he added.

"She always handles me very well," said a voice from behind them as Stephen's hands slid around her waist in a possessive gesture and drew her back against his body. "Don't you, darling?" he added, his lips against her hair.

"Stephen, for heaven's sake!" she said, trying to pull

away. Besides her surprised colleague, several of her students were looking on, clearly fascinated by this evidence of their professor's humanity.

"Ah, I see you were the victim of a bit of mischief-making in there," George said indulgently, his sharp eyes taking careful note of the casually intimate position of Stephen's hands on Viola's body. "You must be the person who's always sending flowers to Viola." He looked more closely at Stephen's face. "Haven't we met before?"

Stephen put out his hand. "I believe you were the moderator of a discussion I took part in a few weeks ago, sir," he said politely.

"This is Stephen Silkwood," added Viola. "The mystery writer."

"Well, well," said George, beaming with paternal pleasure. "And to think the two of you were at each other's throats that evening. Are you walking back to your office, Viola? I'll tag along with you, then. Are you working on a new novel, Mr. Silkwood?"

"I just finished one, as a matter of fact," said Stephen affably.

"You finished it?" Viola cried. "Congratulations! Are you going to take a break now, finally?"

"You got it, Professor," he replied, slinging an arm around her shoulders as they walked down the steps of the lecture hall into the warm May sunshine.

Stephen answered George's questions about his work as they walked together along the red brick pathway that wound across the picturesque New England campus. When they reached the entrance to the old wooden structure that housed the Whittacre English department, George excused himself to hurry after a colleague, saying to Viola, "And to think you've always had such an interest in detective novels. How utterly appropriate! Best of luck, my dear." He rushed off—to tell everyone the news, no doubt, Viola thought.

"You needn't have been so obvious about it," she said to Stephen as they entered her office and closed the door.

"He's the most infamous gossip in the entire school. Now everyone will know we're having an affair."

"Who cares?" he said huskily, drawing her toward him.

"*I* care! It's embarrassing, and besides, I've got a reputation to protect," she added absurdly.

"Ah—the much abused and slandered Desdemona. Reputation? A fig, as Iago says. Come kiss me."

"I will not," she retorted, only half seriously.

His hands slipped around her throat. "Kiss me, darling, or I'll strangle thee."

Giving in, she relaxed under the sensuous pressure of his lips. A shiver of desire ran through her. She leaned back in his arms and grinned at him. "You sound like a sixteenth-century Max Trencher. If I'd wanted someone who could act the murderous Othello, I'd have slept with one of my colleagues."

"But you didn't. You slept with me and sealed your fate. Come on, get your things. It's a lovely day, and it's going to be a fine weekend for some casual love between us."

"You're in a merry mood, aren't you? Well, you may have finished your novel, but I've got exams to prepare. A week or two from now when I'm free, you, no doubt, will be hard at work on your next book," she said, unable to keep a touch of bitterness out of her voice.

He groaned with mock despair. "And never the twain shall meet? We're going to have to do something about this crazy schedule of ours."

"I haven't seen you for ten days," she added reproachfully.

"I know," he said, sidling up against her again and running his lips gently over the line where her hair met her forehead. "Better get me home in a hurry, mate, or I'll rip off your clothes and take you against the desk."

"You're so romantic," she said mockingly, her lips curling in a smile.

The fact was, she reflected, as she packed her things for the weekend, she was still uneasy about her relationship with him. Their acknowledgments of love that night last month in the Hyatt Regency had not led· to what she considered a wholehearted commitment. His work was getting in the way.

Stephen had complained about being unable to write during the week when she had been so determined to break off with him, but as soon as she'd agreed to love him and be faithful, his creativity was revived. "You've inspired me," he told her cheerfully, phoning her from the Cape every night to report his progress with Max's adventures. "The novel is really rolling along."

That was all very well, she'd thought, but it seemed unfair that as a result of her inspiration of him she should lose his company. On the other hand, she had work to do, too. There were classes to prepare, term papers to grade, and, of course, Percy Quentin's biography to finish.

They spent the weekends together, and although their enjoyment of one another continued to be joyous and fulfilling, Viola knew by now that she wanted more. It was bitter for her on Sunday evenings when they had to part. She wanted to stay with him, live with him, sleep every night in his arms, wake every morning to his warm, sexy grin. She was tired of being a weekend date.

She wondered now, as she dropped into her briefcase a paper written by a student who had been coming every week for extra help, if anything would change as a result of the completion of Stephen's mystery. Maybe the novel was just an excuse. Maybe he didn't need her as much as she needed him. It was all too possible that Stephen's idea of being in love was entirely different from her own.

She turned to him, handing him her briefcase to carry. For the first time in several weeks, she noticed, there was a genuinely relaxed look about his eyes. He gave her an enormous grin. He was elated, she realized, and some of his gladness communicated itself to her. She made a mental promise not to do or say anything this weekend to spoil his sense of satisfaction at having finished his novel.

"You got everything?" he asked her, opening the door.

"Yes, I think so. Let's go."

They were walking down the hall toward the exit when an office door opened and David Newstead emerged with an armful of books. Viola blushed. She had explained to David that she and Stephen had worked things out, but she and Stephen hadn't run into him together since that awful afternoon at her house.

Stephen was the first to speak. He started to put out his hand, but evidently thought better of it after another look at David's pile of books. "Hello there. What's all that? You must be researching an entire literary period."

"Just returning books to the library," David said stiffly.

His eyes were for Viola alone. There was a question in them, and she instinctively understood that David was still willing to be her friend if she needed him. She was touched. "Everything's fine," she said softly, answering his unspoken question.

David nodded. "I'm happy for you," he said. He looked at Stephen, seemed about to speak, then changed his mind and cleared his throat instead.

"I know," said Stephen. "She's a lovely lady, and I'd better not let her down. That's what you're thinking, isn't it?"

"Yes."

Stephen's arm tightened around Viola in a gesture that spoke his feelings more eloquently than words. "I love her," he asserted. "Does that make you happy?"

"No. But if it makes Viola happy, I'm satisfied," David said gently. "If you'll excuse me, I want to get to the library before it closes."

Viola wanted to squeeze David's hand to show her affection, but she was afraid to embarrass him further, so she just smiled as he passed them to walk down the hall in the opposite direction.

"Poor chap," said Stephen. "He's obviously crazy about you."

"Don't make fun of him."

His eyes came back to hers without the slightest trace

of levity. "I'm not, I assure you. I pity him with all my heart. But I don't think he would have made you a suitable mate. You're too strong. You'd have walked all over him. No, darling," he continued, his voice playfully sardonic, "you need someone masterful like me. Which reminds me, wait until you see what's happened to poor old Max."

Her attention reverted away from David and back to Stephen. "You mean you're going to let me read it?"

"Only as long as you swoon with admiration. The moment you turn into a literary critic, I'll confiscate the manuscript and make you wait until the book comes out. *If* it comes out," he added as an afterthought. "When she reads it, my editor is probably going to quit."

"Have you got it with you?"

"In the car."

"I'll read it as soon as we get home."

He grinned and moved a hand over her backbone as a reminder. "We have another little matter to take care of first, my love."

She returned his grin and his caress. "First things first, of course," she agreed complacently.

Several hours later, Viola was curled up in one of the easy chairs in her living room with Stephen's manuscript. She was clad in a short terry-cloth bathrobe, and her hair was a wild tangle from Stephen's passionate caresses. He was stretched out on the sofa in front of a blazing fire, which had been kindled less for warmth than for atmosphere. He was naked except for the pair of worn cutoffs he'd pulled on after they'd made love. He was drinking a glass of the champagne she'd opened in celebration of his completion of his novel, watching an old movie on television.

When she first began to read, Viola's attention kept wandering to memories of Stephen's tender lovemaking. But soon the adventures of Max Trencher drew her in completely. There were some subtle changes in the offing this time around, she discovered. For the first time in his eventful life, Max was in love.

The woman was a red-haired gun-control advocate, and although Max had taken her to bed, it was she who had had to make the first move. The heroine had class, beauty, and brains, and Max had been afraid that he'd screw things up if he came on too strong.

Viola couldn't guess how it was going to end. She was ready to be furious if Stephen killed off the heroine. Max wouldn't shoot her this time, but the bad guys might.

As she approached the final pages, Viola began to think that Stephen was going to allow his hero to keep his lover, maybe even to marry her. The bad guys were all shot, beaten up, or arrested, and the heroine was still alive. In the last chapter, Max asked her to marry him.

Viola impatiently flipped a page. The redhead turned Max down. She loved him, she admitted, but as a gun-control advocate, she couldn't reconcile herself to marrying a man who went around shooting people for a living.

The book ended with Max drinking in a bar with his cronies and joking callously about the redhead. "Underneath all that class she was a whore like any other," Max declared. But Viola knew—as every other reader would—that Max was suffering.

She put down the final page and looked over at Stephen. He was staring at the final long shot of Garbo as Queen Christina just as she learns that her lover is dead. She thought she heard him swallow rather loudly. Reaching for a tissue, she wiped her eyes, then tossed the box to him. "You're crying," she accused him as the movie faded out.

He looked over at her, teary-eyed but unembarrassed. "So are you. I thought you were reading my book, not watching the movie."

"I'm crying over your damn book," she admitted. "I feel sorry for Max."

A slow grin lit his face. "You're kidding."

She got up and crossed the floor to the sofa, tears trickling down her cheeks. She sat down beside him and grabbed another tissue. "She didn't have to let him down so hard," she sniffed. "She knew all along that he shot people. Maybe she could have reformed him. Why don't you rewrite the end and let them get married?"

Stephen's fingers slid into her hair on either side of her face while his thumbs rubbed away her tears. "What a romantic you are, darling. Max can't get married. My readers would never tolerate it. He's got to be free to rape more women in his next book. I'm not sure they'll tolerate this much of a soap opera, frankly. My publisher's probably going to reject it."

"No, Stephen, it's good. You saw how I ripped through it. I couldn't put it down. It's more realistic than your others, and certainly less offensively sexist. But it's not as if you've changed your style or anything like that. You've still got your brawls and your bloodbaths and your four-letter words. Max is a little more mellow this time, that's all."

"Yeah, a real marshmallow." He pulled her down across his bare chest, massaging her shoulders through the terry-cloth robe. "You know whose fault it is, don't you? You're a dangerous influence on me. In the next book old Max'll probably find himself out on the pavement parading in support of feminism."

She laughed and bent her head to kiss the rough hairs that sprang from the center of his chest. From there her mouth moved down to one of his tiny nipples, which hardened just as her own did when stimulated. The feel of it tensing under her tongue sent a warm rush of desire through her.

"I love you, Max," she whispered, as his hands swept her backbone more insistently.

"I'm not Max," he said fiercely. He spread his legs enough to pull her in between them so her body was lying the length of his. His aroused state was obvious against her, and this excited her further. He undid the cloth belt at her waist and parted the V of her bathrobe at the collar until her warm breasts tumbled against his naked chest. "I'll prove it to you," he added, his mouth administering a series of short, biting kisses to her lips and throat.

"How?" She was returning his kisses just as tauntingly, allowing him no access to the inner warmth of her mouth.

"Elementary, my darling." He slid the robe off her shoulders, exposing her nakedness fully. She moved up on him slightly so her breasts hovered above his lips. When he tried to reach her with his tongue, she drew back just enough to make it impossible. He smiled, even as his breathing accelerated. "You're going to torture me, are you?" he muttered, trying and failing once again to reach her.

"Long and slowly," she confirmed.

"Two can play at that game, sweetheart," he threatened. The pressure of his hand between her shoulder blades brought her down within his reach, and his mouth captured a nipple and sucked on it greedily. She shivered against him. He changed breasts, gently nipping the second aroused tip with his teeth. She gasped and arched away. "Oh, no, my love," he drawled, pulling her back for more loving punishment. "You began this. Do you dare forget that I come equipped with teeth?" He nipped her over and over until she was shuddering with passion. "And claws." His nails scored her lightly, up and down her back, not hard enough to hurt.

"Brute," she managed. "Do you dare to claim you're not Max?"

"There's a big difference between us, I assure you."

He expertly flipped her over so she was lying beneath him and slid up over her so she could unzip his cutoffs. Her fingers moved furiously at their task, so eager was she to have his naked flesh against her. She guided the blue denim down over his hips, fondling him as she unclothed him, reveling in the feel of his flat stomach, his hard-muscled thighs, his proud masculinity. She crept lower on the sofa beneath his kneeling body, kissing and nuzzling him lovingly while he shuddered in pleasure at the intimacy of her caress. "Oh, Lord, if this is torture, you've got yourself a willing victim," he groaned.

She kept up her warm exploration of him until he muttered that he was losing control and drew back. "I want you to lose control," she said huskily.

"Not yet," he insisted. "Not quite yet, Professor."

He rolled off the sofa and knelt on the carpet with her body stretched before him like a sensual feast. His fingertips moved over her so lightly and slowly that she wanted to scream. Arching her body, she tried to get him to deepen the caresses, but he persisted in the maddening, feather-light stroking. "I once read a book—utter pornography it was—in which the man drove the woman into a state of sensual delirium with the help of a long, pointed feather," he said. "Got any feathers, darling?"

She shook her head. "I'm the one who's supposed to be torturing you, remember? I've never gotten even with you for what you did to me at the Hyatt Regency." She slid off the sofa to join him on the carpet. "Remember the first night you came here? When you so rudely unbuttoned the front of my dress?"

"I'm not likely to forget the thrill of that, moon goddess," he said, reaching out to take her naked breasts between his palms. His thumbs rubbed erotically over the tips. "I also remember lying down on this very carpet with you while you wantonly aroused me. Shortly thereafter, as I recall, you insisted on stopping, you little tease." He bent his head and kissed her breasts slowly and deliciously. "I should have taken you right then and there. I should have established myself as your master right from the start."

"Sexist beast!" she retorted. "Lie down on your back. I'm going to punish you for that remark."

Stephen meekly obeyed. "My blood pressure just shot up about forty points. What are you going to do to me, my fair lady love?"

"I'm going to make you beg for it," she returned, smiling devilishly.

She crawled over him on her hands and knees so he could see her body, but she wouldn't allow him to touch her. Teasingly, she kissed his lips, brushing them with the tip of her tongue. Then she lowered her upper body just enough so that the tips of her breasts grazed his chest. His rough hair tickled her nipples, causing them to harden and swell. When he reached up to touch one of the pointed tips, she pushed his hand away, then grabbed his wrists and pinned them to the floor, as he had so often done to her.

He laughed up at her, his eyes aglow with passion. "Paper tiger," he taunted. "In two seconds I could have you flat on your back begging for mercy."

"Not in this fantasy. This time you're helpless, and I'm completely in control. Do you want me?"

"You know I do, woman."

She shook her head so her hair lashed him back and forth, across his face and neck. Then she lowered her body sensuously along the length of his. Her hips found his hardness, and she moved provocatively against him but deftly avoided his attempts to claim her.

He groaned his frustration, and the sense of power she experienced excited her more than she had ever dreamed it would. "Mmm," she murmured against his lips, "I'm beginning to see why you like this masterful stuff, tough guy. It feels good to see you helplessly writhing with lust down there."

"Just wait," he retorted. "Before this night is over I'm going to keep my long-standing threat to tie you to the brass bed rails and do deliciously evil things to you. When it comes to the masterful stuff, you, darling, are strictly an amateur."

"Oh, yeah?" She found a tender spot on his shoulder and let him feel her teeth. He made a low sound in his throat and arched himself against her, thrusting toward her warm moistness. She evaded him again, laughing softly. "Take it easy, Superman," she whispered. "A woman likes it slow, with lots and lots of preliminaries."

She slid down on him and explored his rock-tense body with a fiery trail of kisses, from his throat to the wide expanse of his chest, softly over his flat-muscled stomach and in between his thighs, where the skin was as soft and tender as her own. His body moved erratically, in little jolts, every time her tongue found a new spot to torture, but she never continued any caress long enough to grant him his release.

He was breathing in shudders when he finally said, in a voice made unrecognizable by passion, "All right, witch, I'm begging. I need you now, quickly. Please."

Her own desires were stoked so high by this time that she was read to comply. Her flesh flowed along him, sinuously as a serpent-woman's, until her thighs were locked against his. Her legs parted for him as she helped him find the place. Then she lowered herself, slowly, onto him.

"Yes, yes," he gasped, wrapping his legs around her to draw her closer. For the first time since she'd started teasing him, he brought his hands into action, stroking her shoulders, her back, and digging his fingers into her bottom. "Sexy lady," he murmured.

For several seconds they lay still. Despite her burning desire, Viola was conscious of a deep sense of ease and peace, merged with him thus, as close as it was possible to be. He, too, seemed to find a momentary relief from his tension, even though fulfillment was yet to come.

"I love you, Viola," he said. "We're perfect for each other, you know that?"

"I know it," she sighed. She withdrew slightly, then rocked back on him until the tenderness in his eyes changed back to desire. He lifted her enough to get his hands on her breasts, bringing her lower body arching more tightly against him as a result. She moaned as he squeezed and tugged on her nipples. Her body began to move with his in an erratic rhythm that quickly built to ragged bursts and thrusts of passion. Viola lost all awareness of her surroundings as she felt herself caught in the grip of an inexorable web of tension, which grew ever tighter and more demanding until it captured her completely and flooded her with pleasure.

Stephen stayed with her, riding the crest just a moment behind her, whispering her name faintly in his usual quiet way as he went rigid in her arms, the pulse in his neck careening wildly against her softened lips.

For a long time afterward they were silent, the silence of ease and contentment with each other. The only sound was the occasional hiss and crackle of the dying fire. Then suddenly Viola raised her head to grin down into his languorous, beard-roughened face, saying, "So there, Max. Your redhead really got you this time. I expect to see masterful women in your novels from now on."

With a quick, devilishly clever motion, he flipped them both over so she was trapped beneath him. She laughed and strained playfully against him, enjoying the still-erotic feeling of his powerful body pinning hers to the thick carpet. His lips feathered her eyelashes, her cheeks, and the corners of her mouth as he said, "I've warned you before—don't get cocky, bright eyes."

"I love you, Max," she responded, kissing him.

"I'm not Max," he said intensely. "Listen, sexy lady, and I'll tell you the real difference between him and me." He paused, his expression becoming very serious and at the same time very loving. "Max's redhead refuses to wed him," he said gently. "Mine, I hope, is going to opt for the happy ending."

Her tongue went thick, and her eyes got round. "Are you asking me to marry you?" she asked, her voice wavering.

"Yes, my love. Will you?"

"Stephen . . ." Her hands slid into the curly black tendrils at either side of his head and held him still, just above her. "You mean it? You want me to share your life, eat with you, sleep with you, live with you in your splendid seaside isolation, be there even when you're writing your precious melodramas?"

"That's what marriage usually entails, I understand," he answered, laughing. "There'll be a few other requirements too, don't forget, such as cooking an occasional meal. You can cook, can't you, darling?"

"Not as well as you," she admitted wryly. "I'm a career woman, remember?"

"Only too well," he sighed, referring, obviously, to her infamous book review. "I'm not asking you to give up your career, love. We'll keep both houses if necessary. I'll live with you in Whittacre during the week, and on the weekends we can escape to the seaside."

"That sounds perfect," she breathed.

"Does that mean you accept?"

"Yes, Stephen, of course!" she cried, throwing her arms around his neck.

He kissed her deeply, and she held him close, hardly daring to believe in her own gladness. "What's the matter?" he whispered, touching his lips gently to her forehead. "There's a frown here." He kissed the spot between her brows. "A worry line, darling?"

"No," she assured him. "A line of amazement, probably." She laughed. "I was beginning to think you couldn't make such a permanent commitment. For the first time I actually found myself envying one of Max's women. She got the proposal I so desperately wanted!" She was no longer afraid to reveal the true depths of her vulnerability. "I love you so much. Sometimes it still seems like a dream that you love me, too."

"Idiot," he said teasingly, the warmth in his sea-green gaze flooding her with reassurance and love. "I knew as soon as I met you eleven years ago that someday you were going to be my partner in life."

"Oh, sure," she began skeptically.

"Really. You had the combinations I couldn't resist, lady. A sweet body and a sharp tongue. Loveliness and wit. Sexiness and a spicy temper. You were a challenge."

"A challenge," she moaned. "I knew it!"

He rolled over and reached for the ice bucket that held what remained of the champagne. Pouring them each a glass, he linked his arm with hers, clinked glasses, and crooned, "To my feisty, fiery lady; may she have lots of red-haired, blue-eyed children to further liven up my life."

"Green-eyed," she corrected smilingly, secretly thrilled at the idea that he wanted children. Her career was important to her, but she knew she could do both, and she couldn't think of anything more wonderful than carrying his child under her heart. "And one or two with black, curly hair wouldn't be bad either," she added, caressing him as she sipped the sparkling wine.

He put his arm around her shoulders as they sat close together and gazed into the glowing coals of the fire. Viola's heart was beating strongly and steadily from pure happiness. She could sense his ease of mind through their wordless mental communication.

"You know what I think we should do for our honeymoon?" he said after a while. "Rent a sailboat for a few days in honor of the afternoon we fell in love."

"Just as long as you don't capsize us again."

"If I remember correctly, you were the bungler who capsized us."

"Me? You're a damned liar, Stephen Silkwood! I'll have you know that I'm an excellent sailor. *You* capsized us. You probably wanted to kiss me and chose that way as an excuse to take me in your arms and—"

He stopped her mouth with a tender kiss. "I've never needed an excuse for that, darling. Stop arguing. I've got a feeling life with you is going to be one long battle."

"Maybe so, but in the long run, as you've proved time and time again, you domineering devil, I usually end up surrendering. After all"—her fingers touched him intimately, teasingly—"you're the one with the sword."

He nodded, his green eyes twinkling. "Just as long as you keep that in mind, Professor." His hands ran over her, peacefully, soothingly, as they held each other close and listened to the shared sound of their heartbeats echoing in each other's breasts. Viola closed her eyes, luxuriating in the feel of him, the loving warmth of him.

She had never felt so at one with any human being before, and he was to be hers, forever.

"You know what?" she said a little while later as they curled up together for the night in her big brass bed.

"Ummm?" He was nearly asleep.

"I think Percy would be happy."

"Yes," said Stephen, his eyes coming open again. "Strangely enough, so do I. Deep down I think he liked me. Deep down I think I wanted him for my own father."

"You're at peace with him now, aren't you, Stephen?"

"I'm at peace with the world," he confirmed, kissing her gently and holding her close until they both fell into the most contented sleep they had ever known.

_____ 07221-4 **CHERISHED MOMENTS #133** Sarah Ashley $1.95
_____ 07222-2 **PARISIAN NIGHTS #134** Susanna Collins $1.95
_____ 07233-0 **GOLDEN ILLUSIONS #135** Sarah Crewe $1.95
_____ 07224-9 **ENTWINED DESTINIES #136** Rachel Wayne $1.95
_____ 07225-7 **TEMPTATION'S KISS #137** Sandra Brown $1.95
_____ 07226-5 **SOUTHERN PLEASURES #138** Daisy Logan $1.95
_____ 07227-3 **FORBIDDEN MELODY #139** Nicola Andrews $1.95
_____ 07228-1 **INNOCENT SEDUCTION #140** Cally Hughes $1.95
_____ 07229-X **SEASON OF DESIRE #141** Jan Mathews $1.95
_____ 07230-3 **HEARTS DIVIDED #142** Francine Rivers $1.95
_____ 07231-1 **A SPLENDID OBSESSION #143** Francesca Sinclaire $1.95
_____ 07232-X **REACH FOR TOMORROW #144** Mary Haskell $1.95
_____ 07233-8 **CLAIMED BY RAPTURE #145** Marie Charles $1.95
_____ 07234-6 **A TASTE FOR LOVING #146** Frances Davies $1.95
_____ 07235-4 **PROUD POSSESSION #147** Jena Hunt $1.95
_____ 07236-2 **SILKEN TREMORS #148** Sybil LeGrand $1.95
_____ 07237-0 **A DARING PROPOSITION #149** Jeanne Grant $1.95
_____ 07238-9 **ISLAND FIRES #150** Jocelyn Day $1.95
_____ 07239-7 **MOONLIGHT ON THE BAY #151** Maggie Peck $1.95
_____ 07240-0 **ONCE MORE WITH FEELING #152** Melinda Harris $1.95
_____ 07241-9 **INTIMATE SCOUNDRELS #153** Cathy Thacker $1.95
_____ 07242-7 **STRANGER IN PARADISE #154** Laurel Blake $1.95
_____ 07243-5 **KISSED BY MAGIC #155** Kay Robbins $1.95
_____ 07244-3 **LOVESTRUCK #156** Margot Leslie $1.95
_____ 07245-1 **DEEP IN THE HEART #157** Lynn Lawrence $1.95
_____ 07246-X **SEASON OF MARRIAGE #158** Diane Crawford $1.95
_____ 07247-8 **THE LOVING TOUCH #159** Aimée Duvall $1.95
_____ 07575-2 **TENDER TRAP #160** Charlotte Hines $1.95
_____ 07576-0 **EARTHLY SPLENDOR #161** Sharon Francis $1.95
_____ 07577-9 **MIDSUMMER MAGIC #162** Kate Nevins $1.95
_____ 07578-7 **SWEET BLISS #163** Daisy Logan $1.95
_____ 07579-5 **TEMPEST IN EDEN #164** Sandra Brown $1.95
_____ 07580-9 **STARRY EYED #165** Maureen Norris $1.95
_____ 07581-7 **NO GENTLE POSSESSION #166** Ann Cristy $1.95
_____ 07582-5 **KISSES FROM HEAVEN #167** Jeanne Grant $1.95
_____ 07583-3 **BEGUILED #168** Linda Barlow $1.95
_____ 07584-1 **SILVER ENCHANTMENT #169** Jane Ireland $1.95
_____ 07585-X **REFUGE IN HIS ARMS #170** Jasmine Craig $1.95
_____ 07586-8 **SHINING PROMISE #171** Marianne Cole $1.95

---

*Available at your local bookstore or return this form to:*

 **SECOND CHANCE AT LOVE**
*Book Mailing Service*
*P.O. Box 690, Rockville Centre, NY 11571*

Please send me the titles checked above. I enclose _____ Include 75¢ for postage
and handling if one book is ordered; 25¢ per book for two or more not to exceed
$1.75. California, Illinois, New York and Tennessee residents please add sales tax.

NAME_____

ADDRESS_____

CITY_____STATE/ZIP_____

(allow six weeks for delivery)                                    **SK-41b**

# WHAT READERS SAY ABOUT
# SECOND CHANCE AT LOVE BOOKS

"I can't begin to thank you for the many, many hours of pure bliss I have received from the wonderful SECOND CHANCE [AT LOVE] books. Everyone I talk to lately has admitted their preference for SECOND CHANCE [AT LOVE] over all the other lines."
  —*S. S., Phoenix, AZ**

"Hurrah for Berkley . . . the butterfly and its wonderful SECOND CHANCE AT LOVE."
  —*G. B., Mount Prospect, IL**

"Thank you, thank you, thank you—I just had to write to let you know how much I love SECOND CHANCE AT LOVE . . . "
  —*R. T., Abbeville, LA**

"It's so hard to wait 'til it's time for the next shipment . . . I hope your firm soon considers adding to the line."
  —*P. D., Easton, PA**

"SECOND CHANCE AT LOVE is fantastic. I have been reading romances for as long as I can remember—and I enjoy SECOND CHANCE [AT LOVE] the best."
  —*G. M., Quincy, IL**

*Names and addresses available upon request